Amber

Amber

Julie Sykes

First published in 2014 by Curious Fox, an imprint of Capstone Global
Library Limited, 7 Pilgrim Street, London, EC4V 6LB
– Registered company number: 6695582

www.curious-fox.com

ISBN 978 1 782 02059 2
17 16 15 14 13
10 9 8 7 6 5 4 3 2 1

A CIP catalogue for this book is available from the British Library.

Main cover image: Shutterstock © oliveromg
Background image: Shutterstock © Anatolii Vasilev

Typeset in Perpetua 13pt.

Printed and bound by CPI Group (UK) Ltd, Croydon, CR0 4YY.

For Alistair, Antonia, Will and Tim

ONE

Sunlight shone through the window. It warmed my face and imprinted small red circles behind my eyes. It had to be time to get up, but waking was such an effort. To drag my body into consciousness felt physically harder than swimming underwater. It was tempting not to bother, but I had a nagging sense of things to do. With an effort, I forced myself awake.

What was I wearing? Still dizzy with sleep I stared in disbelief at the hideous garment that I was dressed in. The effort was too much. I shut my eyes and let my head weigh heavy on the pillow, until my brain caught up with the rest of me. For an unnerving moment I couldn't place where I was. The room smelled unfamiliar; its hard, antiseptic odour stuck in my throat and made my head swim with the memory of something frustratingly just out of reach. I prised my eyes open and stared around. I'd expected to see... suddenly I wasn't sure what I'd expected, but it wasn't this plain white room, with minimal furniture and no personal stuff.

So where was I exactly? And more to the point how did I get here? I sat up and winced as a pain seared through my head. What had I done to deserve that? It must have been something pretty spectacular judging from the state I was in. My body ached; it felt like I'd been hit by a bus. I gingerly pushed back the thin grey blanket and stiff white sheet beneath it.

'Hi there, how are you feeling?'

A middle-aged woman, large and homely, dressed in some kind of uniform, stood at the end of the bed. She was making notes on a piece of card. She smiled warmly, as if she was genuinely pleased to see me awake.

My face burned. How long had she been standing there? I brushed the back of my hand across my mouth, wiping away the drool seeping from the corner.

'Okay, I think.' It was a lie, of course, but what else could I say? 'Thirsty,' I added croakily.

The woman came forward and poured me a glass of water from a jug on a locker next to my bed. 'Here, sip this. Not too much at first.'

As she passed me the glass our two hands met. Her rich skin, the colour of polished wood, made mine seem pale and ghost-like. The water tasted wonderful. I sipped slowly, fighting the urge to gulp it down in one go.

'Better? Good. I'm Kirsty, your nurse. What's your name?'

I opened my mouth, then stopped. Good question.

What was my name? I closed my eyes while I hunted in the depths of my mind for an answer. My name? Come on, it wasn't a hard question. But my head was empty. It felt like an enormous void.

'Um,' I flushed, feeling stupid. 'I can't remember.'

There was concern on Nurse Kirsty's face. She quickly hid it with a bright smile. 'Never mind! You'll remember in a minute. Do you know where you are?'

'Hospital?' It didn't take a genius to work that one out.

'That's right. This is the Rowan Bank hospital near Kirkgreen, in Scotland. Your accent's not local. Are you on holiday?'

So many simple questions and not one answer! I gripped the sheet as I fought to control the panicky feeling swelling inside me.

'I don't know,' I whispered. I bit my lip. I was not going to cry. I'd embarrassed myself enough already without adding tears to the experience.

'Don't worry, love,' Kirsty gave me another of her reassuring smiles as she squeezed my hand. She reached for a small rectangular box attached to the belt on her uniform and pressed a button. 'Doctor Poole asked to see you as soon as you woke. He'll be here in a minute.'

Kirsty held on to my hand until the doctor arrived. It felt weird, because I didn't know her, but I didn't want her to let go. She chatted away in a light, undemanding tone. She didn't seem to expect a response and she didn't ask me any questions. I was grateful. Kirsty's voice was soft and her accent on the vowels seemed different to mine. I let her conversation roll over me like waves breaking on a beach. Was I on holiday? If only I could remember something about myself. Anything! It didn't have to be my name. Right now I'd settle for my dress size, or favourite type of food or anything to help fill this big empty space in my head.

Doctor Poole was short and bearded but what he lacked in height he made up for in presence. Kirsty bowed her head as he marched into the room. In a matter of seconds he'd felt my forehead, shone a torch into my eyes, listened to my breathing and checked both my pulse and blood pressure. He was clearly a man who didn't waste time. I had a vague recollection of having had a similar sort of check-up not so long ago, but I couldn't remember where or why. Finally, the doctor handed me a mirror saying, 'Don't worry about the black eye. It won't take long to heal. It looks a lot worse than it is.'

My heart raced as I lifted the mirror. I couldn't wait to see myself. Then the memories would return. They had to because it wasn't possible to forget your own face. Or was it? I stared eagerly at my reflection. The bruise ringing my left eye was something to be proud of. It would definitely get noticed at…

As I let my gaze flick to the bigger picture my throat constricted. A girl with long chestnut hair, a straight fringe dusting the dark eyelashes of hazel eyes, stared back at me. She had high cheekbones and clear skin that was tanned and healthy looking. She was about sixteen years old. Terror engulfed me. The girl was a stranger.

Doctor Poole broke the silence. 'What's your name?' he asked casually.

I couldn't manage speech so I shook my head.

'Do you remember anything about yourself? How about your age? An address? Or maybe the number of people in your family?'

The questions were easy, nursery school stuff. So why, instead of answers, was there a blankness, thicker than fog, smothering my consciousness?

Doctor Poole turned to Kirsty and said quietly, 'Nurse, did the patient have any personal effects on her?'

'Yes!' Kirsty went to the locker. She pulled open the top drawer and brought out a necklace and a slim, black, rectangular object. She held them out to Doctor Poole, who nodded for her to pass them to me.

'Do these mean anything to you?'

I took the things eagerly and placed the black object

on the blanket while I transferred the necklace to the flattened palm of my right hand. I stared at it for ages. I sensed that it was special and wished that I could connect with it. The golden chain was as delicate as a spider's web. From it hung an irregularly shaped amber stone, with a zigzag of gold through the middle. The colour of the amber made me think of the setting sun. It was achingly beautiful. I longed to try it on but hesitated. I felt like a thief. Did the necklace really belong to me?

Kirsty must have guessed what I was thinking. She leaned in and, sweeping back my hair, deftly fastened the chain around my neck. 'There you go.' As she stepped back she added, 'That's so pretty.'

The moment the necklace touched my skin my fingers were drawn to the amber stone. They traced around the outline then moved on to the surface. It was cold and smooth to my touch. I loved the feel of the raised lightning-shaped bolt of gold that almost split the gemstone in two. Someone had taste. Had that someone been me, or was the necklace a present? I let it go reluctantly as I reached for the rectangular object. It was almost the length and width of my hand, with rounded corners and a slightly curved back. The surface was lighter and looked like it might be a screen of some sort. It had a round button at one end and there was a thin switch on the top edge.

The device felt solid but it wasn't heavy. I turned it in my hand, knowing that it was significant.

Doctor Poole thought so too. 'It's a mobile phone. It should list your contacts. Switch it on and we'll take a look.'

A mobile phone! Well, at least I knew what that was. I pressed the round button, then jabbed at it impatiently when nothing happened. I tried the switch at the top. The phone remained lifeless.

'It's run out of charge. Nurse, do you have a phone like that? Can you lend...' Doctor Poole paused. 'Can you lend the patient a charger?'

'Sorry doctor, my phone's so cheap it practically came free with my cereal,' Kirsty answered.

The patient! How long would it be before I remembered my name?

Kirsty was ahead of me. 'Would you like to choose a name, love, just until you remember your old one? I'm sure it won't be for long.'

Doctor Poole nodded his approval. 'Good idea,' he agreed.

I didn't want a new name but I didn't want people to call me 'the patient', either. So what should I call myself? My hand strayed to the necklace. It was all I had, that and the mobile phone. Two small things that linked me to a life

13

I couldn't remember. It wasn't much, but it was a start.

'Amber,' I said.

'Good choice,' Kirsty beamed at me. She wrote it on the white card, quickly, as if she couldn't bear for me to be 'the patient' either.

'What happened? Why am I here?' With a jolt I realised that no one had said. The doctor and Kirsty exchanged a look. I could tell there was worse to come. My heart plummeted as Doctor Poole lowered his voice in the annoying way adults did when they were delivering bad news. 'There was an accident. The car you were travelling in was hit by an articulated lorry.'

'Oh!' That explained a few things. I had a sudden, uncontrollable and totally inappropriate desire to laugh. I breathed deeply. As I inhaled, a sharp pain wiped the smile clean from my face. My hand flew to my chest and I slowly let the breath out again.

'That's bruising,' said Doctor Poole, in a matter-of-fact voice. 'We X-rayed, and you haven't broken anything.'

They took X-rays. I wrapped my arms around my chest. It made me feel even more vulnerable knowing that Doctor Poole and his medical team had examined me when I was unconscious.

'The accident, was I driving?' Could I drive? I didn't remember.

Doctor Poole and Kirsty exchanged another look. Before I had time to process what it could mean Kirsty held my hand again.

'You were a passenger,' said Doctor Poole, his voice strangely soft. 'You're lucky to be alive, very lucky. Another motorist, and his son, pulled you free from your car just seconds before it exploded.'

'My car exploded?' I didn't do things by halves then. But I was only the passenger.

'What about the driver?' I asked.

'She was a woman; unfortunately she... she perished in the accident.' Doctor Poole paused.

I stared at him. I had a question, but the words stuck in my throat.

A sympathetic look flashed across Doctor Poole's face. 'We don't know who the lady was. She might be related to you. Then again, she might not. The accident only happened last night. Your travelling companion was burned so badly there was little to go on. We've established that she was probably in her early thirties. My own daughter's sixteen. You look a similar age. It's possible that the driver was your mother, if she was very young when she had you. I'm sorry but, for now, that's all I can tell you.'

The shock was like a punch in the stomach. I clutched at Kirsty's hand as I fought to breathe. Surely this couldn't be happening?

'I really am very sorry.' The words were a cliché, but Doctor Poole spoke them kindly enough.

Anger burned me. I didn't want sympathy. It wouldn't bring my... who though? Was the driver my mother, a sister, or a friend? I wished she was here and could tell me. A sadness that was colder than winter crept over me and snuffed out my anger. Questions crowded in my head. Did I live round here, or was I passing through? Where had I been going? I reached inside myself, searching for answers, but it was no good. No matter how hard I struggled to recall them, the details of my life weren't available.

'What's wrong with me? Why don't I remember anything?' I hadn't meant to sound aggressive, but fear made it come out that way.

Doctor Poole shifted on his feet. For a moment he looked uncomfortable. 'What do you know about retrograde amnesia?'

TWO

Retrograde amnesia. I'd heard of that, but as I struggled to remember what it was, Doctor Poole explained. 'Retrograde amnesia is a condition that's often triggered by a traumatic event. It leaves the sufferer with no memory of their past. All their personal details are lost, although many people can remember previously learned skills, like driving a car, speaking a foreign language or playing an instrument.'

He sounded like he was quoting from a medical dictionary.

'Is it permanent?' I asked. My breath caught in my throat. I wasn't sure I wanted to know.

'That depends. It doesn't have to be, but every person is different. Some people never get their memories back. Others find that, after meeting family and friends, sharing photographs and handling familiar possessions, they do start to remember some details of their life. The important thing is that everyone is different. You have to go at your own pace. Don't let anyone rush you.'

No chance of that. No one knows who I am. That left a bitter taste in my mouth. How come no one had realised that I was missing? Surely I wasn't a total loser? I had to have some friends other than the woman driving the car – the woman who might be my mother. I blanched and frantically tried to un-think that, in case just having such a thought could make it come true.

'Do you have any more questions?'

Yes. Who am I? I shook my head impatiently.

'The good news is that you're fit and healthy in every other way.' Doctor Poole continued talking to me. Every now and then he'd slip in a personal question, making no comment when I couldn't answer it. At last he said, 'You look tired. You should take a wee nap.'

I forced a smile and weakly shook the hand he offered me. As he left the room with Kirsty, I slid down the bed and pulled the sheet up to my nose. I was tired and my head hurt. I longed to be able to start again, to close my eyes and wake up with my identity intact. Sleep eluded me; my brain buzzed like an orchestra warming up for a concert. My fingers strayed to the necklace. *My necklace.* It was comforting to know this was part of my forgotten past. It was a small but crucial piece of an enormous jigsaw that had come without a picture to help me work it out. A thought dropped into my head and my heart raced. The rush of excitement it gave me was greater than if I personally had discovered the atom. I was the one with the answers.

What I didn't have, just yet, was the key to unlock them. Or did I? I sat up eagerly. Where was that mirror Kirsty had given me earlier? I scanned the room until I spotted it, on the shelf near the door. At once I swung my legs out of bed and, placing my feet on the floor, tried to stand. I hadn't expected my head to spin one way and the room the other. I clutched at the bed's metal frame and hoped that I wasn't going to throw up. So maybe I wasn't quite ready to go jogging yet. When the room stilled and I stopped feeling like I was going to heave my last meal, whatever that had been, I sat up straight and tried again.

It was no good. I was weaker than a new butterfly. Maybe I had enough strength to bring the mirror to me though. One by one I relaxed my muscles. I started with my toes and gradually worked my way along my feet, and then up my legs to my abdomen. I followed this by relaxing the muscles in my torso and arms. Next I worked on my neck and head until every fibre in my body was so chilled that you could have stored *gelati* on it. Even my breathing had taken on a slow easy rhythm. Finally, I reached out with my mind and engaged the mirror. I grasped it firmly and forced it to rise up from the shelf. The mirror slowly glided across the room towards me. I knew I was grinning like an idiot, but I didn't care.

Closer.

I guided the mirror over the bed and when it was an arm's length away I plucked it from the air. There! That was one thing I hadn't forgotten. In triumph I held the mirror up to my face. I'd taken the first step on my journey of self-discovery. Then, frustratingly, the journey stalled. I'd hoped that when I saw my reflection again it would trigger a rush of memories. Wrong! It was still the face of a stranger, staring back at me. I gazed at the mirror for ages. I couldn't believe that I was the girl in the reflection. I checked out every centimetre of her face. I stared into her eyes, admiring the pale green specks that flecked the hazel. I wondered at the amazing length of those dark eyelashes. I noticed the small brown mole to the side of her mouth. The girl in the mirror was pretty, even with a black eye, but I didn't know her.

With a deep sigh I sent the mirror spinning through the air to the bedside locker. As it spun I flipped it, so that it landed propped against the wall where I could see it. I looked at it often, turning my head quickly in its direction, as if by sneaking up on my reflection I'd catch it out and remember who I was. But the girl in the mirror was faster. She never gave anything away.

As the day progressed there were more visitors. First a

cheerful orderly with the lunch trolley – he demanded a smile in exchange for a meal. His friendly banter made me laugh and I willingly traded a smile with him. Not that I ate much of the food. I had little appetite. I picked over the tuna salad and barely touched the strawberry cheesecake. A social worker called Nicky came next. She was eager to discuss what would happen to me once I was discharged from hospital. It was hardly a discussion. My fate had been sealed when Doctor Poole realised that my phone had no port for a charger and was a fake, or not a phone but something else. Either way, all hopes that it would reveal my identity were dashed.

'We don't have much to go on,' said Nicky.

She clutched at a thick wodge of paper. I couldn't help but raise my eyebrows. If that wasn't much it was just as well there wasn't a lot to go on.

'Doctor Poole thinks that you're sixteen, so we have to treat you as a minor. It means you'll be placed in a foster home. It's only a temporary measure,' she added, catching my grimace. 'We've got to act quickly. Your injuries are superficial. You're almost ready to be discharged.'

Superficial! Was this woman serious? I wouldn't call an event that wiped my brain so clean that I didn't even know my name, superficial.

Nicky caught my expression. 'Your physical injuries,'

she added quickly. 'We can arrange for you to see a psychiatrist as an outpatient.'

Great! I didn't bother to argue. I didn't need a shrink. My head was empty, not messed up. Let them book me an appointment. By the time it came round I might already have the answers I craved. I had my sights set on the small black gadget now lying in the top drawer of my locker. I had a strong feeling that it would tell me more about my life than any shrink doctor.

The social worker bulldozed on, asking me questions about the type of foster placement I'd prefer. My response was less than helpful, but how the hell was I supposed to know what sort of family I wanted to lodge with: big, small, with pets or without? Nicky could place me with foster parents from another planet for all the difference it would make to me right now. Then there was the solicitor.

'I don't need one,' I said decisively when Kirsty announced his arrival.

'Of course you do,' she'd answered as she plumped my pillows and smoothed my hair. 'How are you going to cope if that was your mother in the car? Yes, they're putting you in temporary foster care now, but what happens when you turn eighteen? You'll need somewhere else to live and that requires money. You're owed compensation.'

At first sight Mike Saunders, the solicitor, looked

scarily official but actually he was very nice. He didn't use baffling legal jargon and he didn't talk down to me when he was explaining my rights. But when he casually asked, 'So you can't remember your real name?' I froze. It was like I'd been dunked head first into a bucket of *sleeta*. Fear prickled my spine. An image flashed into my mind of a woman, smartly dressed, pointing to a computer presentation projected onto a clean white wall.

NEVER tell them your real name. Forget how nice they are. It could cost you your life.

I acted on instinct, forcing myself to relax and squashing my rising panic to a place so deep that I couldn't feel it any more. The woman's voice continued to play in my head, low and urgent.

Tell them anything personal and we're all as good as dead.

'No, I'm sorry,' I shrugged, helplessly.

Mike didn't even raise an eyebrow. 'There's nothing to be sorry about,' he said. He continued to make notes on a large pad, covering the pages with his deft strokes in black pen. I watched, my expression neutral, even though my insides were tighter than the laces of Mike's shiny black shoes. Finally he stopped writing and, delving into his jacket pocket, he pulled out his card. 'Keep in touch. I need to know where to find you.'

'I'll do that.'

The moment he'd gone I dropped the card on the bed, scared that by touching it I could give away something that was strictly classified. I couldn't help the nervous laughter that burst from my mouth, but silenced it quickly. What was going on? Had that been a flashback? Did it mean anything or was my mind broken – crushed in the accident like the car I'd been travelling in? I sat for ages, just staring at the white walls, while I searched in my head for answers.

A long while later I tried to get up again. This time I made it as far as the window. I gazed out, leaning on the sill to catch my breath. I was on the second floor and my room overlooked a car park. It was lined with trees and their outstretched branches were green and lush. It had to be summer I decided, as I watched a woman, dressed in shorts, walk towards the hospital building. My room was air-conditioned but the woman, who looked fresh and summery, made me feel hot and uncomfortable. My hair itched and I suddenly longed to take a shower.

To my embarrassment my gown wasn't secure and the tied back gaped as I walked, revealing bare skin underneath. I crossed the room and opened the door by a crack to spy on the outside. No way could I go any further if there were other people around. Just as I was inching the door wider, someone pushed it from the other side.

My arms flew round me, gripping the gown in place.

'Going somewhere?'

'Kirsty!'

My breath rushed out in relief.

'It's lovely to see you up but I need to do your obs. Sit down there for me.'

She shepherded me over to the chair, barely waiting for me to sit before she stuck a digital thermometer in my mouth. She laid her fingers on my wrist and took my pulse.

'Can I have a shower?' I mumbled, as I tried not to bite the thermometer or spit it out.

'Of course! I'll find you a towel and some soap in a minute.'

'Have I got any clothes?'

'Stop talking or it'll take longer.'

When the thermometer beeped Kirsty removed it. She squinted as she read the number display. 'Normal. Good girl! Right then, clothes next. We ditched yours. We had to cut them off you, but there's usually some spare stuff hanging around. Lost property and items that people have donated. I wonder what size?' Head tilted Kirsty pursed her lips while she looked me up and down.

'Hmm, I bet you're a ten. Wait here and I'll see what I can do.'

While I waited I wondered if anyone was missing me. Perhaps someone was calling all the local hospitals right now and it was only a matter of time before they discovered I was here and came to get me. I wished they'd hurry up. I didn't want to stay in hospital. I needed to be with people who knew me. Then my memory might return.

Kirsty came back. She struggled through the door, pushing it open with her hip, as her hands were full. I went to help her.

'Is all this for me? Thanks.'

'Don't thank me until you see what's there,' Kirsty answered mildly. She dumped everything down on the bed. 'It's not Prada.'

'Prada' didn't ring any bells, but I didn't say anything as I sorted through the pile of clothes. Eventually I chose a plain blue T-shirt – misshapen and faded from too many rides in the washing machine, a grey hoodie – with the number 18 stitched on it in red cotton – and a pair of jeans. There were two bras, so I took the smallest, and there was also a brand new packet of underwear. There was no choice of footwear, just a hideous pair of fluffy slippers that would have looked great if I was going all out for the yeti look. Kirsty had also found shampoo, half a bottle of conditioner, a bar of soap and a tube of toothpaste.

'Some of this is stuff is new,' I said pointing at a hairbrush and the toothbrush, still in their original packaging.

'I went to the shop in the lobby.'

'Thank you.' It seemed inadequate and Kirsty's kindness made me suddenly tearful.

'It was nothing,' she said gruffly.

Kirsty dug out a hospital towel and took me along to the shower room. It was an antiquated, windowless box. It took me ages to work out that instead of waving my hand across the dial I physically had to turn it to get the spray to work. With the door shut, and the shower pounding hot water over me, it wasn't hard to imagine I was the only person in the world. I guess in many ways I was, at least in my world! The thought filled me with white-hot panic. I slammed it away. I refused to believe that no one was missing me.

It was strange to see my body for the first time. I was covered in bruises and had a long red welt that ran diagonally from my neck across my chest, where the seat belt had restrained me. It was sore and I washed carefully to avoid the bruising. I finished by shampooing and conditioning my hair. I stood under the shower, loving the tingling sensation as the water cascaded over me. It was the first thing I'd really enjoyed since I'd woken. It was only when the skin on my fingertips began to wrinkle that I reluctantly turned off the shower. I squeezed the excess water out of my hair by winding it in my hands, and then towelled my body dry on the scratchy hospital towel. That was a novelty too. Had I gone back in time, or hadn't they got people driers in Scotland yet?

I was much happier now I was clean and ready to face whatever came next. My first challenge was dressing in the cramped shower room without slipping on the damp floor. I leaned my shoulder against the wall as I wriggled into my underwear and then the jeans. The bra was on the generous side and the jeans far too loose around the waist, but both were a vast improvement on the hospital gown so I wasn't complaining. When I was fully dressed, I stood and brushed my teeth at the tiny sink. I collected up my toiletries. As I padded back along the corridor the yeti slippers made loud slapping noises on the polished floor. When I reached my room I saw a group of people gathered inside. I stopped and my heart thudded loudly.

A picture was forming in my head. It was so vivid that for a moment I swear I caught a whiff of perfume as the woman from my earlier flashback materialised. The woman's face was in close up, her brown eyes intense as she pressed the point home.

NEVER tell them your real name.

The picture faded and I wanted to run away. Only it was too late. The people in my room had seen me.

THREE

'I'm sorry. We startled you.'

I stared nervously at the family gathered by my bed. There was a man, a woman and a boy who looked about the same age as me. The woman continued speaking but I could hardly hear her above the noise of my heart thundering against my chest. I breathed deeply until I felt calmer. I felt awkward as I studied the people. Did I know them? Were we related? I looked at the boy from under my long fringe and my heart skipped with relief. His name was… it was there, on the edge of my tongue. Come on, what was it now? The boy was cute. He was a head taller than me and built like an athlete. He had bright blonde hair and the most amazing blue eyes. He saw me staring and smiled. My heart sank. I didn't know him and the name I'd sought dissolved, leaving me with the sour taste of disappointment.

I smoothed down my damp hair self-consciously. 'Hi…' I hesitated. 'Do I know you?'

'We're the Marshalls. I'm Mia, this is my husband, Jeff, and Daniel, our son,' Mia Marshall reached out as if she was going to take my hand. She hesitated then let her arm drop back to her side. 'Jeff and Dan were travelling behind you when your car got hit.'

My insides somersaulted. 'You pulled me out!'

'Dan did. I went for the driver, but the belt was jammed…' Jeff's voice cracked. A haunted look crossed his face and I guessed I wasn't the only one having flashbacks.

There was a silence. Finally I couldn't bear it any longer. I had to know.

'What did she look like?' I asked. 'The driver, I mean.'

'I don't remember. It all happened so fast and it was dark.' Jeff shook his head. 'Short hair, I think. She was a wee lass, I could have easily lifted her, but I couldn't get her out.'

'You did what you could.' It sounded ungrateful. 'Thanks,' I added. 'And thanks for helping me.' I glanced over at Dan.

He nodded then looked away quickly, as if being a hero embarrassed him. I racked my brains for something to say, to break the awkward silence, and caught sight of my huge yeti feet. What if he thought these were my own clothes? Now I was the one who was embarrassed. Totally tongue-tied, I ran a hand through my hair exposing my black eye.

'Ouch! That looks sore. Dan got a black eye just like that a few months ago,' Mia volunteered.

'How did it happen?'

'Sailing. I got smacked in the face by the boom. The wind was gusting and I wasn't paying attention. I was lucky – I almost went overboard.' Dan's blue eyes twinkled mischievously as he remembered.

I smiled and suddenly felt more relaxed. Dan opened his mouth to speak, but Mia got in first.

'We run the Waterside School of Music. It's near Kirkgreen. Maybe you've heard of us?'

I shook my head. 'So you're all musicians?'

Mia nodded. 'I play flute and the piano. Jeff plays piano and violin, and Dan plays the saxophone. What about you, do you play an instrument?'

'I...' I paused, wondering if I did.

'Sorry, daft question! Look, if you're staying in the area, please drop in and see us. The nurse said they're nearly ready to discharge you. Do you know where you're going yet?'

'I think they're still working it out.'

'Oh, I see. Well, you could...' she hesitated. Then she reached out and patted my arm.

'It's going to be fine. Foster care won't be for long, a few days at the most. Your real family will come for you soon.'

If I have any family left. I faked a smile and wished

that my eyes would stop welling with tears every time someone was kind to me. Mia tactfully changed the subject. I gradually relaxed and became less tongue-tied. The Marshalls seemed nice. They were quiet, clearly not wanting to seem too cheerful, given the situation, but they were open and friendly. Their visit passed quickly. All too soon they were saying goodbye. Dan gave me a friendly grin, Mia hugged me swiftly and Jeff shook my hand. When they had gone I felt even lonelier than I had before. I sat on the bed and stared miserably at the stark white walls. All the questions that I'd tried so hard to avoid swarmed into my head like maggots invading an apple.

The nurses changed shifts. Kirsty came to see me before she went home and brought me a bundle of magazines that she'd swiped from the staff room. 'Take care. I'll see you tomorrow.'

With nothing better to do, I flopped on top of the bed and flicked through the magazines. They weren't very interesting, but I kept reading in the vain hope that something in them might spark a memory. If anything the magazines scared me even more. How could I not recognise any of the current fashions, or the names and faces of the hottest celebrities? I hadn't even known the year we were in until I saw it on the cover of one of the magazines. It made me feel out of touch, like I'd been living somewhere else entirely.

A long while later, a girl wearing a green auxiliary's uniform came round wheeling a beverages trolley. She opened the door, holding it with her foot as she called, 'Anything to drink?'

I sat up self-consciously, pulled down my T-shirt and pushed back my hair. The auxiliary looked amused. She patted her own honey gold hair, caught in a chic knot at the nape of her neck, with a carefully manicured hand. She was ultra-poised and wore her drab green uniform with the confidence of someone who knows she'd look good dressed in anything.

'What is there?' I asked.

'Tea, coffee, hot chocolate or hot milk.'

'Er...' Did I like any of those? 'Tea, please,' I said, opting for the first thing on the list. 'I haven't seen you before. Have you just started your shift?'

The auxiliary expertly manoeuvred her trolley into the room and began to pour tea from an urn into a mug. 'I'm a volunteer. I do three nights a week – it'll look good when I apply for university. I've just finished my first year at college.'

'That sounds great. I'm Amber, by the way.'

'I'm Holly Jenkins. Great's not the word I'd use,' she said, dryly. 'But I suppose it could be worse. My friend

34

volunteers here too and she got geriatrics.'

Holly was too busy checking me out, her lips curving up at the sight of my second-hand clothes, to notice the yeti slippers I'd abandoned in the middle of the floor. She tripped over them as she brought the drink to my bedside. 'Eek!' she squealed.

The hot liquid splashed over her hand and she dropped the mug. It must have hurt quite badly because she didn't stop it, even as the mug plummeted closer to the floor. I relaxed my body and then fixed the cup with my mind. I held it in the air until the tea stopped sloshing about. It felt good. I made the mug hover in front of Holly, smiling broadly at her as I waited for her to take it from me. But there was no nudging of minds to show that Holly was ready. Then I noticed that she'd turned whiter than the room. She was clearly in no state to help. Concerned that the burn might be serious I moved the mug to the drinks trolley. I put it down slowly to avoid spilling what was left of the drink. Holly stared straight at me, and not in a friendly way either.

'Sorry, did I do something wrong? You didn't mind me helping, did you?'

Holly's eyes bulged and I wondered if she was having some kind of fit. She grabbed the trolley and screamed like she was being mugged.

'What?' I jumped off the bed, but I still couldn't see what the problem was.

'Get away from me.' Holly continued to scream. She bashed the trolley into the wall as she reversed it from the room. I was impressed. Who'd have thought that one person could make such a noise? Holly, unbelievably, could scream louder, and did just that when the wheel of the trolley locked up. The door swung open and a nurse rushed in, snapping on rubber gloves, ready to deal with the emergency. She was very unimpressed to find me alive and well.

'What's going on?' she asked, her voice steely.

Holly tore her eyes away from me and shrieked, 'She's weird!'

'Excuse me?' The nurse's face darkened.

'Sh-she's weird,' stuttered Holly, nodding in my direction.

My face burned with embarrassment. Since when had helping out become weird?

'I tripped... it... it... I dropped the tea,' Holly struggled to get her words out. 'But it didn't... she... she made it float... in the air! It was freaky.'

The nurse stared at me. My head whirled. Suddenly I was transported back to the room with the smartly dressed woman from my previous flashback. She was giving a presentation on a computer. Her elfin face, framed with short dark hair, was friendly enough but her brown eyes were hard and calculating as she delivered her message.

Lie if you have to.

Her steely tone made my toes curl.

Too bad if it causes trouble. It's them or us.

She paused and looked around. I got the impression that she was lecturing to a group, although I couldn't see anyone else in the room.

Never forget, our world is in your hands.

The words echoed in my head. I was hardly aware that I'd leaned forward in an effort to learn more. I almost howled with frustration as the image died abruptly, like a mobile phone out of charge. Blood pounded through my ears. My head ached with the pressure of it. I forced myself to stay calm and appear normal.

'What do you mean?' I looked Holly straight in the eye. 'You caught the mug! It was brilliant. I bet you're great at netball.'

Holly took a step back, shaking her head, a mixture of fear and something indescribable in her eyes. The nurse tutted crossly. 'The patients are waiting for their bedtime drinks. And when you're done Holly, I'd like a word. Hurry up, now.'

Holly shot me a look of pure venom. She darted forward and slammed a mug of tea on the locker, and then bolted out of the room with her trolley. I let my breath rush out in a sigh. This situation was getting more surreal. Was the safety of a whole world really in my hands? It had certainly felt that way a moment ago. But surely I couldn't be that important?

I felt like I'd been catapulted into a crazy game without being told the rules. Rule one, I'd just discovered, almost to my cost, was not to move an object without actually touching it. I cupped my hands round the mug of tea and lifted it to my lips. Had that always been a rule? Moving things with my mind felt as normal as breathing. Clearly it wasn't, so was this talent something I'd previously kept a secret? Or was it something new? Maybe the accident had altered me? If a traumatic event could steal away my memories, then anything was possible. I sipped at the muddy brown liquid and nearly spat it straight out. It was an effort to swallow as I placed the mug back on the locker. Now I had rule number two. Never ask for tea again. It tasted disgusting.

That night I slept so deeply that when I woke it was almost too painful to bear. Here I was, still trapped in the same scene. My fingers strayed to the amber necklace. They stroked the smooth surface first, and then sought out the band of gold zigzagging down the middle. I knew the necklace was special, but whatever secrets it held were tightly trapped inside the red-gold stone.

Trapped like me! Suddenly I couldn't bear to be in bed for a moment longer. I threw back the blanket and got up. I wrenched off the uncomfortable hospital gown and pulled on my second-hand clothes. Then, after making my bed, I went along to the shower room to wash and clean my teeth. Breakfast arrived, delivered by the same orderly that I'd met yesterday. I gave him a smile, without being asked, and sat on the chair to eat.

A while later Kirsty came in to do her morning observations. 'Are you after my job?' she asked, eyeing the neatly made bed.

I was reading a magazine and I pushed it aside as I opened my mouth for the thermometer.

'I can't stay here forever.'

'Something tells me that won't happen. Nicky rang. She's on her way to see you. She's got you a placement.'

My stomach fluttered anxiously. I didn't want to stay in the hospital for a second longer than I had to, but did I really want to go and live with a family I didn't know?

The placement turned out better than I could have imagined. As Nicky bounced into my room she waved yet another sheaf of papers at me. 'It's good news. Mia and Jeff Marshall have offered you a place at their music school. Strictly speaking it's not a foster placement, but given your circumstances it's got to be better for you. We're going to relax the rules if you'd like to go there.' Nicky thrust the papers into my hands. 'I got this from the Waterside School of Music's website. It should cover everything you need to know, but ask me if it doesn't. Waterside runs a special summer school from June to August for students aged from eight to eighteen. Everyone eats together in Melody House – that's the main building – but as an older student you'll sleep in a log cabin, with twenty other girls. There's music tuition in the morning and sport in the afternoon. When I spoke to Mia she was easy about that. She said that during your stay, you're to participate in as much or as little as you want to. She also said to tell you that you're welcome to live as one of the family. The Marshalls have a flat in Melody House, but she thought that being a part of the summer school might be less intimidating. So what do you think?'

What did I think? My heart soared. It was a great idea. I liked Mia and her family, and even though I'd still be living with strangers we wouldn't exactly be on top of each other. There'd also be lots of people my own age around. If I was busy making new friends, and getting on with things, my memory might come back. Learning an instrument sounded fun and then there was all the sport, if I was there long enough of course.

'How long can I stay for?'

'As long as you need to,' said Nicky, barely concealing her relief that I'd agreed so easily. 'Mia was quite definite about that. She wants you to treat Waterside like your home. Although I'm sure it won't be for more than a few days. Someone must know you.'

Home! The wave of sadness that hit me was worse than a physical pain. Had I been travelling with my mother? I didn't remember. Knowing that we might never meet again was more than I could bear.

'There's some paperwork to complete before the hospital can discharge you, but I'll take care of that while you pack.' Nicky reached for her briefcase, pulled out a carrier bag and handed it to me. 'I brought this to put your things in.'

What things? All I had were the toiletries Kirsty had given me. I took the bag and thanked her. Then I went and found Kirsty to say goodbye. She wrapped her arms round me in a bear-like hug. 'Don't worry, pet. It's going to work out fine. A pretty young girl like you, someone knows who you are.'

It took seconds to throw my possessions into the bag.

I couldn't sit still and went to the window to look out. A man was walking through the car park with a mobile phone clasped to his ear. With a jolt I remembered my phone or whatever it was. I couldn't believe I'd nearly left it behind. I spun around and fixed my eyes on the bedside locker. I held the top drawer with my mind and tugged it open. It slid effortlessly, allowing me to transfer my thoughts to the object lying inside. With one fluid movement I lifted it up and directed it to the carrier bag, but as I was about to drop it inside I changed my mind. The device felt too important to chuck in a bag. Instead I brought it towards me and, releasing my mind grip, pulled it from the air.

The gadget was solid yet light. As I curled my fingers around its curved back something shifted in my mind. A memory slowly began to surface. When I tried to retrieve it the image flitted just out of reach. The harder I tried to recall the memory the blacker my mind went. Frustration welled inside me. I sighed as I tucked the gadget into the pocket of my jeans.

The door opened and I jumped guiltily as Nicky breezed in. 'I'm done. Get your shoes on. You're free to go.'

'These are all I've got,' I said, pushing the yetis with my foot.

'I've got a spare pair of trainers in the car. They should

fit you. You can have them. You can't arrive wearing those furry things. We don't want Mia changing her mind and withdrawing her offer to let you stay indefinitely.' Nicky chuckled.

If I don't watch the mind stuff Mia won't let me stay, full stop! I smiled weakly as I headed for the door.

FOUR

My feet slowed as I crossed the car park to Nicky's small red car. I don't mind admitting it, I was nervous about the journey. Would it bring back memories of the accident? I sincerely hoped not. I'd got enough to deal with already. It turned out that my knowledge of cars was patchy. I knew to wait while Nicky unlocked the doors with an electronic key, but I struggled to fasten the seat belt. She leaned over, showing me how to pull the belt out of its plastic housing. She stretched it across my body and clicked it into a special fixture on the floor.

'Ready?' She shot me a friendly grin as the engine leapt to life.

My mouth was too dry to reply, so I nodded.

The hospital was on a main road that ran through open countryside. Everything seemed extra bright and colour-rich after my clinically clean hospital room. Nicky switched some music on and the tune was catchy but unfamiliar. She sang along and I tapped out the beat with my fingers. My head swivelled from side to side as I absorbed the scenery. I'd hoped that I might recognise something, anything, but there was nothing memorable about the route or the small volume of traffic using it. We reached a town and the road became much busier. I held my breath, full of respect, as Nicky navigated the narrow streets that threaded their way between tall stone buildings. The architecture was quaint, but I hated it. The cramped streets seemed to suck the air away and made me feel breathless. It was a relief when we left the town behind. The traffic faded as we drove further into the countryside, passing by fields full of fat white animals with funny, flat faces. Low hills scrolled across the horizon, their barren slopes littered with rocky outcrops. A short time later our journey was over. I wasn't sorry. The seat belt was chafing my bruises and I ached all over.

'Nervous?' asked Nicky as she turned into an unmade drive. Two wooden posts, with a bar across the top, supported a white sign that read 'Waterside School of Music'.

'A bit.' An understatement; tiny birds were swooping in my stomach.

Nicky drove along the bumpy drive. Sunlight filtered through the trees, dappling the road with patches of gold. It was extremely peaceful. For a moment I forgot about the dull ache in the pit of my stomach. I filled my lungs with the sweet woodland air and committed it to memory, along with the view. There was a huge black cavern in my head. I hoped these new experiences would help to chase away the darkness. The road curved sharply, the trees to my left thinned to reveal an enormous expanse of water that shimmered invitingly. Taken by surprise I gasped out loud, 'A lake!'

Not that the clue wasn't in the name, the *Waterside* School of Music.

'Pretty, isn't it? We call it a loch up here in the north. You can do all sorts of water sports at Waterside, including sailing. You should try it.'

'Maybe.' I hadn't meant to sound unenthusiastic. Skimming across the loch in a boat sounded great fun, if that's all you had to worry about. I touched my amber necklace. Not knowing who I was, or where I'd be now if I hadn't had an accident, made me feel restless. I wanted to be doing something to learn my identity.

The drive looped again, to the left this time, and opened into a car park. Beyond it stood a graceful, two-storey house built from an orangey pink stone. It had a pointed roof with decorative gables and a tall, ornate chimney. To its right, and set back, was a similar but smaller building and beyond that a collection of brick built buildings and wooden cabins. Several cars were parked nearby and anxious parents were helping their children to unload an assortment of luggage and musical instrument cases. I glanced down at my one crumpled carrier bag. At least I wouldn't have to waste time unpacking.

'Today is change-over day,' Nicky explained as she parked the car.

'Change-over day?'

'Summer School runs for the whole of the holiday, but the majority of students just stay for two weeks, arriving and going home on the Saturday. That's today. Mia tells me this is the start of week three.'

All at once I was overcome with shyness. Everyone looked so confident and many of them knew each other, judging from the amount of screaming and hugging going on. Even those students who were here for the first time shared one thing in common with the regulars. They all played a musical instrument. I didn't even know if I liked music.

Nicky threw me a sympathetic look. 'You're going to have such fun,' she said brightly. 'But you can call me if it doesn't work out for you.'

'You won't forget me, will you? You'll go on trying to find out who I am?' I hated how needy I sounded.

'Of course! We're doing everything we can. Right now we're checking the missing person's database to see if anyone's looking for *you*. We're also making enquiries in England. Your accent's so hard to place. We wondered if you might have travelled up from the south. Then again, you could be from Europe. Someone knows you and...' Nicky paused, 'your travelling companion. You won't be here for long. It's only a matter of time before people start asking where you are.'

As I climbed from the car I slipped my hand into my pocket to touch my mobile phone. Its smooth surface, solid against my fingers, gave me hope. It wasn't a fake. I *sensed* it. It was the key to my past. All I needed now was to find out how to unlock its secrets.

Several adults with clipboards stood around. They were dressed in black polo shirts with the school's name neatly embroidered in gold letters on the left side. They directed everyone to the smaller of the two buildings. Nicky walked on past them.

'Mia told me to come to Melody House. It's where she and her family live. It's also where the students have their meals.'

I followed her up the steps to the front door and stood awkwardly while she rang the bell. As we waited for someone to answer I realised that I was looking forward to seeing Mia again. Imagine if I'd had to go and live with someone I'd never met before. When the door swung open I was touched that Mia seemed pleased to see me and hugged me like an old friend.

'Hi there, you found us then. Welcome to Waterside. You're going to have such fun here. I know it! I've put you in Chopin, our cabin for the older girls. Most of the students have to share a room, but there are a few singles. I've allocated you one of those, but if you'd prefer some company then I can change it.'

'A single's great, thanks.'

'Good,' Mia smiled. 'Let's get you settled and then I'll give you the tour. I've got your timetable here, but apart from meal times, feel free to ignore it. You don't have to join in with any of the activities.'

I glanced at the piece of paper she handed me. Breakfast was early, which suited me fine. Along with group practice, I'd been given a private music lesson every morning except for Saturday. Afternoons were dedicated to sport. The evenings were free time but there were lots of organised activities too. It sounded pretty intense, but I wouldn't be bored.

Chopin was set apart from the other cabins. It had its own little garden and there were a couple of wooden tables and benches. My room was on the first floor, at the end of the corridor and opposite a bathroom. It was small but comfortably furnished. It had a single bed, a wardrobe and a chest of drawers. There was also a tiny dressing table with a mirror, a desk and a chair. The walls were pale yellow and the blue and white curtains and bright, multicoloured rug on the floor gave it a homely feel.

'We'll need to get you some things,' said Mia, eyeing my carrier bag, 'How about a girly shopping trip this afternoon?'

I hesitated. Something was stirring in my mind, but before I could work out what was bothering me it slid away. 'That'd be great, thanks.'

'Don't worry about the money,' Nicky interjected. 'We'll make sure Mia is reimbursed.'

Money! That was it. I didn't have any of my own.

'No problem,' Mia was unconcerned. We'll leave when lunch is over. Now that you've seen your room, how about I show you the rest of the campus?'

Nicky skipped the tour because she had another appointment to go to. Before she left she handed me a card with her direct line number. I tucked it in my pocket along with the one from my solicitor. At this rate I was going to need an address book.

The Waterside School of Music was set in sixty acres of scenic woodland, so Mia proudly informed me. Most of the buildings were clustered around the south side of Loch Calness. There were eight log cabins divided equally between boys and girls and segregated by an infirmary and the water activities centre. Meals were taken in the main building, Melody House. A smaller building, Mahler, was the office, where you went to adjust your timetable, sign in and out of school – older students only – and pick up parcels. Not that anyone would be sending me a parcel. There were courts for netball, basketball, volleyball and tennis, and football and rugby pitches. On the east side of the complex, just past the boys' cabins, stood the Bluewater Concert Hall. It seated an audience of 260 and also housed a function room and several practice rooms.

'And now for the *pièce de résistance*,' said Mia. She led me through the woods to a beautiful building with a spectacular open-air stage, right next to the loch. 'The Margaret Becker Memorial Building and Stage,' she said proudly. 'Margaret Becker was a friend and a composer. She loved it here. When she died she left us a significant amount of money for the advancement of music. We used it to build this. It's such a shame that she never knew about it.'

'It's beautiful.' The building seemed familiar and I immediately connected with it. Tingles raced down my spine. Had I been here before? I didn't recognise the woods or the stunning backdrop of Loch Calness. Maybe I'd seen pictures of the building in a brochure or something. My mind ticked over so fast I almost could hear it processing. Was it possible that I'd been on my way to Waterside when I'd had the accident? I shook my head, checking my thoughts before they ran away with me.

Mia was watching me. 'Are you feeling all right?' She patted my arm. 'Do you need to sit down? I almost forgot that you were only discharged from the hospital this morning.'

I pulled myself together. 'I'm fine. Can we go inside?'

'Yes, of course, it's this way.'

We walked round the back of the concert stage to double-fronted glass and wood doors. Mia pulled one open and as she ushered me inside I was met with a refreshing blast of chilled air.

'There are state-of-the-art rehearsal rooms, ensemble practice rooms, a function room and a recording studio.'

We walked down a bright corridor with doors leading off to both sides.

'These are the practice rooms.' As she passed each door Mia glanced in through the glass window. She stopped outside a room numbered '5' and gestured for me to look too.

I leaned forward and saw Dan blowing into a gold-coloured instrument with a long curved neck. His blonde hair was rumpled. The muscles in his tanned arms tensed as his long fingers worked a shiny set of keys and his body swayed to the music. He looked up suddenly and raised an eyebrow at me in a friendly gesture. My heart flipped as I smiled shyly back. Did he realise how attractive he was? But I was staring! I pulled away from the door quickly.

'What is that instrument?' I asked, glad that my voice sounded normal even though my heart was thumping.

'Saxophone. Want to go in and give it a try?'

'N-no,' I stuttered. How awkward would that be?

Luckily the door to Room 7 opened and a girl about my age, with shoulder length strawberry blonde hair and wide green eyes, came out.

'Hi, I'm Lucy,' she said with a smile. 'I've been keeping an eye out for you. It's Amber, right? Mia's told me a bit about you. She said we were going to be neighbours. Mine's the single room next to yours in Chopin. I live locally, but I'm staying for the whole of the summer holidays. My parents are musicians. They left me here when they went on tour. So if there's anything you need then give me a call.'

'Thanks,' I said. I liked Lucy immediately and racked my brains for something friendly to say back. 'What instrument do you play?'

'Flute.' She pointed into the practice room.

I followed her line of direction to a chair, next to a music stand. A silver instrument lay on the seat. It was long and sleek with a mouthpiece at one end and a set of raised keys. My fingers suddenly itched to pick it up. I entered the room, unaware that I'd moved.

'You play?' asked Lucy. 'Do you want a go?'

I reached the instrument and lifted it reverently, holding it with both hands. The metal was cold and very shiny but it wasn't pure. Somehow I could tell it was an alloy, probably silver nickel. The keys weren't quite right either. They were slightly closer together than was normal. Then I realised the whole instrument was shorter than it should be, so maybe that was why.

'*Fluetto*,' the word popped into my head and was out of my mouth before I could stop it.

'Flute,' corrected Lucy. 'Or *fluetto*, I guess. What language is that? It sounds Italian.'

I jerked my head round in confusion. 'Sorry, I… flute,' I had no idea where that word had come from.

'Play something,' said Lucy. She gave me an encouraging nod.

Even as I was shaking my head, the words forming on my lips to tell her I didn't know how to, my hands were behaving independently and raising the *fluetto*, no flute, to my mouth. It felt like I was out of my body and watching from afar. The metal mouthpiece reached my lips. I took a deep breath and exhaled softly across it. The note resonated around the room, low and clear. Lucy's grin almost reached her ears. I launched into a series of scales hitting several bum notes as my fingers adjusted to the slightly cramped spacing. It didn't take long to get the hang of it and then I moved on to a simple tune that repeated itself. When I finished Lucy clapped and Mia called out, 'Don't stop.'

I couldn't have stopped playing, even if my life depended on it. My fingers had taken on a will of their own and they danced along the keys, playing songs I didn't know. It was fantastic. The tunes stirred something deep inside me that lifted me so high it felt like I was flying. I played on, tunes that were fun and light, until I realised I was warming up to play something much bigger. Soon my fingers felt supple and my breathing controlled. I knew I was pitch perfect. Then, with the briefest of pauses, I began to play a special piece. It started with three low, mellow notes. The notes hung in the air, hooking the audience and forcing it to listen. As the last opening note faded, my fingers quickened and I blew faster. The tune skipped around the room. It was light and captivating and filled me with a wild happiness. Images flittered through my mind so rapidly they blurred together. The tune danced on until finally it soared to a pitch that made me think of crystal. I held the note and then let it go quickly. As it tumbled down I imagined water splashing over rocks, a breeze fresh on my face and my body floating gently towards the sweet-smelling grass. I knew I was playing the last few low notes of the music. They were the same ones that I'd started with.

I lowered the flute slowly and, smiling at my audience, I dipped my head in a modest bow. Inside I was singing. For the first time since I'd woken up in hospital, I felt truly alive. On a total high I fixed my mind on the flute, grasped it firmly and asked it to rise from my hands.

What was I doing?

The thought slammed me like a punch in the stomach. They didn't do that here. I swallowed my panic as I dropped the flute back into my trembling hands. My eyes flew first to Mia and then to Lucy. Incredibly, neither of them had noticed me trying to pass the instrument back to Lucy with my mind. Lucy was staring at Mia with her mouth open as if she'd lost the power of speech.

'Wow!' she said, at last. 'That was brilliant. She hit C8. Only a professional flautist can get C8 on a standard flute.'

'Amazing,' breathed Mia. 'The music was beautiful… fun, yet haunting. I can still hear it playing in my head. Did you compose it? It's not something that I recognise.'

'Me neither,' Lucy gave a low chuckle. 'It's not a piece you're likely to forget.'

'I-I don't know.' I was dizzy with pleasure. The music was still inside me; it had touched parts of my consciousness that I wasn't aware existed. I felt like I'd been to a faraway place. I had no idea where but it was so good that I wasn't ready to come back. I swallowed and quenched the longing before it devoured me. I handed the flute, as Lucy had called it, back to her.

FIVE

That afternoon Mia took me to Kirkgreen, the local town just a fifteen-minute drive away. She treated me like a surrogate daughter and bought me everything I would ever need – and a few more things for good measure. After a few shops, though, my enthusiasm waned and my smiles became fake. I hated the enclosed feeling of the town, with its narrow streets and grey stone buildings, and longed to be back at Waterside. Shopping depressed me. The boutiques were full of the same clothes, just all in different sizes. Why anyone would want to dress the same way as someone else was beyond me. Clearly it was the norm here though. So, was this a clue to my previous lifestyle? Were my clothes tailor-made? Or had the accident left me with a whole new personality?

Most of the clothes I chose were casual, but Mia suggested I got a straight black skirt, a simple open-necked blouse and a pair of low-heeled shoes, just in case I was still there for the first concert night.

'We stage one mini-concert, to enable some of the short-term students to play for their parents. There's no pressure. It's generally a fun evening. At the end of the summer we hold a larger, formal concert. It's a prestigious event and open to the public by ticket. Many of the local dignitaries come along. The chairs are fixed, and there's a lot of competition for the principal seats. At the formal concert everyone dresses in evening wear. There's also a dinner dance afterwards.'

'Chairs?' I asked.

Mia smiled apologetically.

'Sorry, I just assumed that since you can play the flute your musical knowledge must have returned. Chair order is a kind of hierarchy. First chair goes to our best player, chair two to the second best, chair three to the third best.' Mia started to say something else then laughing lightly she said, 'But I mustn't run away with myself.'

'Sounds fun,' I answered, even though my chest had tightened. I didn't want to be here at the end of the summer and still not know who I was.

We finished our shopping with the purchase of a dark blue holdall, to pack my new things in when I finally left Waterside. Then Mia took me to a small café for a drink. I sipped thoughtfully at an ice-cold Sprite. It seemed a mighty big coincidence that I'd been travelling in the area of the music school before my accident when, as Mia embarrassingly kept repeating, I was a maestro on the flute. There was also the sense of connection that

I'd experienced when I'd first seen the Margaret Becker Memorial Building and Stage. Why did I think I knew it? I'd almost finished my drink before I plucked up the courage to ask Mia a question that had set me on fire.

'Have all the new students arrived?'

Mia looked up sharply. She raised her coffee cup to her face and viewed me over the rim. 'We're still waiting for a couple more. Tom Cooper's parents called to say he's going to be late and will arrive tomorrow. We haven't heard from Erin McKeever yet.'

I was about to ask what instrument Erin played, but Mia swiftly turned the conversation to something else.

Erin McKeever. On the way home I silently repeated the name to see if it rang any bells. It meant nothing. Erin McKeever's life was as big a mystery to me as Amber's.

The accident must have taken more out of me than I'd realised; I was exhausted after the shopping spree. I went to my room, intending to chill out with one of the novels Mia had bought me. Only I couldn't settle. One thing I was learning about myself was that I was a tidy, organised person. It was impossible for me to relax with a heap of carrier bags waiting to be unpacked. I checked the door was locked before I used mind control to put my new things away. I took childish delight in watching my outfits swoop ghost-like across the room. I made each new shoe hop under my bed, to join the yetis I'd been given by Kirsty at the hospital. I could chuck those out now; I wasn't ever going to wear them again. One at a time I made each yeti walk to the bin, giggling at how silly it looked. It amused me so much that I made one slipper tap out a mad yeti dance on the floor. That had me in hysterics. But when it came to it I couldn't throw the slippers away. Call me sentimental, but the yetis were a part of my new history. They could sit on the windowsill, like ornaments. My eyes flicked between the slippers as I decided which one to move first. Before I could choose I felt a weird sensation in my head. My right hand flew to my temple. It felt like my mind was splitting. It didn't hurt. The sensation was more of a tugging, like the feeling you get when you tear wet paper in half. Then suddenly the two sides of my mind began to work independently and I found I could control both slippers at the same time. I lifted them up and made them glide slowly across the room to the window, where I brought them down to the sill. It was incredible.

I had to lean over the desk to arrange the slippers. The view from the window was amazing. I hadn't realised that I could see the loch from here. It looked so peaceful that I had a sudden longing to walk around it. I glanced at my new watch. There was still plenty of time before dinner to go out and get some fresh air. As I came out of my room, Dan and a giggling Lucy came towards me along the corridor. They both had their arms full. Dan carried a rectangular-shaped metal box and a bundle of wires, and Lucy was holding a screen. Dan looked uncomfortable, but Lucy was clearly enjoying herself.

'Hi,' she said, her green eyes sparkling impishly.

'Hi,' I replied. I wondered if Lucy and Dan were going out. Lucky her if she was! Dan was lovely. There was something about him that made me feel as if we'd been friends forever.

'We've brought you a present. We've got to be quick, though. Boys are forbidden in the girls' cabin. Dan's got special permission to be here, but he has to be gone before everyone returns from the welcome meeting.'

'It's a PC,' said Dan. 'It's mine. It's an old one, so you can borrow it for as long as you like. I thought it might be useful for, well you know, surfing the internet.'

Internet... I racked my brains until suddenly I had it. The internet was a global system for carrying a vast range of information and services. It also provided electronic mail. Wow! Add techno geek to music maestro. I was turning into a real nerd. No wonder my friends weren't queuing up to find me. Maybe I didn't have any!

'Thanks,' I said, flushing a little.

'Do you want me to set it up? I bet you could do it, but it might be quicker if you let me as it's my machine.'

'Yes, please,' I said, pushing open my bedroom door.

There wasn't much space with the three of us in the room. I stood watching from the doorway while Dan arranged the metal box, or tower as he called it, under the desk and the monitor and a keyboard on top. When he had connected everything together he plugged it in.

'There's no spare printer,' he apologised, as the monitor blinked to life. 'But I'll lend you a memory stick to transfer data and then you can print from my mine.'

'Thanks,' I was itching to get started and couldn't wait for the computer to warm up. It took forever, but at last a picture of an incredible building set alongside a river appeared on screen. Over the picture, on the left, was a block of icons arranged in a column.

'What is that place?' I asked, hardly able to take my eyes from the picture as I moved closer. The building was like nothing I'd seen before. It was several storeys high with hundreds of tall windows arranged in lines with geometric precision. The stonework was old and intricate and the building had castle-like turrets and a huge clock tower.

'It's the Houses of Parliament, in London,' said Dan sheepishly. 'And that's the Eiffel Tower, in Paris,' he added as the picture changed to a weird metal tower. 'I set my screen saver to places of interest around the world.' He hesitated before adding quietly, 'They're all places that I want to visit.'

'Are you taking a gap year to travel?' Lucy grimaced and then added, 'Good for you, even though I'm done with travelling forever. My parents have carted me around the world at least six times.'

Something inside me went click and a shiver of excitement coursed through my veins. It was like a small part of me had woken up. I liked to travel too. I was sure of it.

'That sounds great. How long until your gap year?' I smiled at Dan.

Dan seemed almost shifty when he replied. 'I'm seventeen. I've just finished my first year at sixth form, so I've got another year left. If I defer university, I could take a gap year next summer. You can change the screen saver if you want,' he added.

'I like this one,' I said. 'Remind me, which icon for the internet?' My hand hovered over the screen.

Dan leaned over me and his arm lightly brushed mine as he reached for a smooth, plastic object with two buttons alongside the keyboard. The contact made my arm tingle. I swallowed and forced myself to concentrate on what he was saying.

'Nothing as flash as touch screen. It's a good old-fashioned mouse.' Dan moved the mouse and an arrow appeared on screen. He held it over a symbol in the shape of a large blue 'e' then clicked the left-hand button twice.

'Double click,' I whispered as my knowledge of PCs flooded back.

'You know what you're doing then?'

'Yes, I'm fine now.'

'Well, just yell if you want help. Or ring me. Have you got a mobile? What's your number? I'll ring you and put my number on your phone.'

I hesitated. Should I show Dan and Lucy my mobile and ask if either of them knew how to work it? But that would delay Dan even further and I didn't want to get him into trouble if the girls came back. Now I had a computer I could work out the phone by myself.

'I don't know my number.'

Dan stared at me sympathetically. 'I'll lend you one. We've a spare kicking around at home. It's not high spec. You can't get the internet on it, or apps, but it works all right as a phone.'

Dan and Lucy left and I sat down at my desk. My hand curled round the plastic mouse. Now I had a whole virtual world at my fingertips there was so much that I wanted to explore. First though, I would research my mobile phone. There had to be some kind of online technical support for it, or maybe a forum where I could ask questions about it. Of course, it might not even be a mobile phone. If that was the case, I fully intended to find out what it was. I dug it out of my pocket and held it in my hand. I examined every centimetre of its smooth, black surface. It struck me that unlike the computer my phone had no manufacturer's name or identifying logo. One side was noticeably lighter. It had to be a screen, and the button beneath it an on-off switch. But when I pushed the button nothing happened. I experimented with different types of touch. Jabbing didn't work, nor did depressing the button slowly. I tried pushing it in and holding it down for several seconds, but that had no effect either. A combination of short jabs and slow pushes also drew a blank.

I breathed deeply. Then I went through the same routine with the thin switch on the gadget's top edge. Nothing! The phone remained lifeless. Well, sort of, because handling it had given me a strong sense of self-importance. How embarrassing! Who did I think I was – a junior spy or something? I laughed at my wild imagination. The flashbacks that I'd experienced previously couldn't have been real. I bet they were caused by the stress of being in hospital and not knowing who I was. I put the gadget on the desk and studied it objectively. It had to be out of charge. So how did you charge a phone with no ports to plug a wire in? Unless...

I leaned over the computer and held the phone up to the window. The screen glowed eerily; it had to be solar powered. I tilted it towards the window to let it catch more of the light. When I pressed the button again the phone remained lifeless.

'Pleeeeaaase work,' I said, as if begging was going to help.

I held the phone to the window until my arm ached so badly that I was forced to put it down. It looked exactly the same as it had before. I wiggled the computer mouse to get rid of the screen saver then typed, 'How to identify your mobile phone' into the box of the search engine.

Two seconds later I had a page of suggestions. My pulse quickened as I scanned the list. All the results were about how to identify your mobile phone's model number. I tried again, this time asking how to identify the manufacturer of your mobile. This list was longer but just as unhelpful.

I guess it was a pretty stupid question to ask. How could you not know what sort of mobile you'd purchased? There was only one thing for it. I would have to trawl through every single manufacturer until I found the mobile that matched mine. My eyes were blurring when, ages later, Lucy knocked to ask if I wanted to walk over to Melody House with her for dinner. It would have been nice if there'd been more to show for my efforts, other than a sore neck and aching shoulders, but there was always tomorrow. I switched off the computer with relief and pocketed my mobile.

SIX

The dining hall in Melody House was a beautiful wood-panelled room, with a crystal chandelier and huge doors that opened on to the garden. We joined the queue for food, served from a series of portable heated food trolleys. I didn't recognise any of the dishes and ended up having the same as Lucy. We collected cutlery from a dresser and then carried everything over to a free table. Lucy sat down and I took the chair opposite her.

'Mmm, lasagne's my favourite,' she said. She broke a roll in half and mopped up some of the sauce. Lucy was clearly someone who enjoyed food.

It was the first time I'd felt truly hungry since I'd woken up in hospital and I set about the meal with enthusiasm. It was delicious. I copied Lucy, mopping up the sauce with my bread. We ate in companionable silence until a prickling sensation down my neck warned me of someone coming up behind me. At once an image burst into my mind of a clean white room, with no more than sixteen desks and a large screen hung at the front.

Never let down your guard.

The voice was cold and uncompromising.

The next thing I knew, I'd spun round and jabbed my assailant in the stomach with an elbow. He uttered a surprised grunt then he doubled over and dropped his tray on the table with a clatter. The water jug rocked and Lucy reached out, her green eyes wide, as she stopped it from tipping over.

'That was friendly.'

To my total mortification, Dan was staring down at me with a mixture of amusement and respect in his eyes.

'Hell! I'm sorry. I didn't realise… I mean, I thought…' I was confused and appalled. What had that been about? My reaction was hardly normal for a sixteen-year-old school kid. Perhaps that spy theory wasn't so mad after all.

Luckily Dan found the incident highly amusing and he burst out laughing. 'Remind me not to approach you on a dark night! That's a pretty mean weapon you've got hidden in your elbow.'

'I'm sorry.' My face flamed. I wanted to run away and hide, possibly forever, but I forced myself to meet Dan's eye. 'Did I hurt you?'

'No,' he chuckled. 'And more importantly, my dinner survived. I was going to ask if this seat was taken, but maybe I'll find somewhere else to eat.'

'I can move if you want to be with Lucy.' Embarrassment

was making me gabble.

'I came to sit with you. Probably safer if I move to the other side of the table though, where I've a better chance of anticipating your next move.' Dan's blue eyes crinkled with amusement as he slid into the seat beside Lucy. She was doubled up with laughter. It took her ages to calm down, and even then the odd giggle kept escaping, like a hiccup, from her lips.

Dan attacked his lasagne with a fork. 'A wee birdie tells me that you're a hot shot on the flute. I'd love to hear you play.'

'Really?' I smiled. 'Not scared that I might beat you over the head with it?'

Dan grinned back at me. 'I have a pretty thick skull. So is that a yes?'

'It would be, but I don't actually have a flute.'

Dan raised his eyebrows. 'And that's going to be a problem here? Mum said she's going to lend you one of hers. Very generous, considering she only has three hundred spare ones.'

'Really!' My eyes widened. Dan snickered and I suddenly realised that he was teasing me. 'How about I play for you tomorrow?' I asked him. 'My timetable says that I have a music lesson first thing, followed by orchestra and a small group ensemble at 11.30 a.m. I thought I'd give the ensemble a miss.'

'Eleven-thirty's good for me too,' said Dan. 'I'll book a practice room out to you. Would you prefer one in Bluewater or Margaret Becker?'

'Margaret Becker,' I said immediately. I might not remember the old me, but this new one definitely knew what she liked best. Or was it just the old me surfacing? There was something about the gracefully curved, open-air stage of the Margaret Becker building that tugged at my heart.

'Good choice! Becker's my favourite too,' Dan seemed pleased and we shared a smile.

'Has Erin McKeever arrived yet?' I asked.

'No,' Dan's expression was guarded. It made me wonder if Mia had been speculating about Erin too. 'It's not that unusual for students to turn up late without their parents warning us.'

There was an awkward silence. Dan finally broke it. 'There's a volleyball match tonight down by the loch. It'll be fun. You should come.' His gaze took in Lucy then lingered on me.

'Sounds great,' said Lucy as she scraped the last bits of food from her plate.

Reluctantly I shook my head. I vaguely remembered the game of volleyball, and I'd have liked to take part, but it had been an incredibly long day, packed full of new experiences. I couldn't cope with any more. My eyes felt heavy and I longed for bed. Just thinking about it set me yawning.

'Thanks, but I'll give it a miss. Another time though.'

'I'll keep you to that,' Dan agreed.

My first orchestra session took place in the Bluewater Concert Hall and was led by an older man with greying hair. He was called Peter Lassiter. He was dressed casually in jeans and a blue Waterside polo shirt. Lucy pointed it out and said, 'The teachers here wear different coloured tops according to their roles. Music teachers wear blue; sports teachers, red; and the domestic staff, black.'

'Why?' I asked.

'To help you to identify each member of staff and their job,' said Lucy patiently.

I still didn't get it. It was easy enough to work out who the staff were because they were so much older than the students. Surely you could ask them what they did. I was going to pursue it but Peter started the session by tapping on his music stand to get everyone's attention. He spent most of the time getting to know us by asking questions about what music we liked and which instruments we played.

'He seems nice,' I said to Lucy, after we were dismissed.

'Yes, well. Don't be fooled. He is nice, today. When we start making the music he will be different,' said a girl with glossy brown hair, filing out of the hall alongside me.

'Claudia!' Lucy darted round me and the two girls hugged.

'Amber, this is Claudia Bergmann, from Munich. She came to summer school last year. Claudia, this is Amber, she's new.'

'Hello,' said Claudia. 'I am very pleased to meet you.'

'Me too.' I sidestepped to let someone pass.

'We are causing the traffic jam,' said Claudia, her clipped accent very different to Lucy's soft Scottish one. 'I will see you both at lunch, yes?'

'Definitely! I've got a lesson now, Practice Room 4. Where are you going Amber?'

'Margaret Becker.'

'Want any help getting there?'

'I should be fine.' My long-term memory might be broken, but the short-term one was exceptionally good.

Dan was waiting for me outside the Margaret Becker building. He was leaning against the wall and had a black rectangular case dangling from one hand. His blonde hair was dishevelled, like he'd got up in a hurry and forgotten to comb it. When his bright blue eyes met mine it made my heart race. He pushed himself upright and held out the case. Our fingers brushed as I took it from him. Sparks skittered up my arm. I pulled back awkwardly. Dan didn't seem to notice. 'You're honoured,' he said smoothly. Mum's lent you her second-best flute.'

'No pressure, then.'

'None needed. According to Mum, you could make music playing a stick.'

I blushed. 'I'm not that good.' Dan raised a sceptical eyebrow and my stomach skipped. 'Really, I'm not.' I protested.

Dan held the door open, letting me go through first. He then led the way along the central corridor to a practice room at the end. My hands shook as I laid the flute case on a table and opened it up. Mia's flute was exquisite, a beautiful work of art with gold-plated keys. I couldn't wait to play it. My fingers twitched with impatience as I slotted the pieces together. Dan sat down on a chair to watch. I lifted the flute to my lips and played my first experimental notes.

'It's good. It has a lovely tone.' The keys still felt in the wrong place but my fingers were adjusting to them. After a few warm-up exercises I moved on to some simple tunes. I ran through the same repertoire as I had yesterday and added a new song that my tutor, Mr Mason, had taught me earlier.

'Not bad,' said Dan, when I finally stopped. He sounded unimpressed but, from the twinkle in his eye, I guessed he was only teasing me. 'You get extra points for playing without music.'

'I can't read it!' The music scores were as unfamiliar as a foreign language. Mr Mason thought that I probably did know how to read music but had just temporarily forgotten.

I played some more songs before I started the special one. The song with the melody that had haunted me since I'd first played it yesterday. I blew softly across the mouthpiece, filling the room with mellow notes. The opening bars faded and Dan leaned forward, a reverential expression on his face. I let the music carry me with it. It lifted me up, tantalising my senses with its magic, until I was sated and ready to burst with happiness. When the finale came, the notes reaching a crescendo and then tumbling down like a spring shower, I glanced over at Dan. His eyes were closed, and his tanned face glowed.

It's a love song. From nowhere the thought dropped into my mind. I tried to catch it but it slipped away, sinking like a pebble in water, leaving me with memories more vague than ripples.

'Wow,' Dan's voice was barely a whisper.

I was embarrassed, and busied myself disassembling Mia's flute. The urge to use my mind was strong and it was hard work resisting it. With slow, exaggerated movements I laid the pieces in the case, closed the lid and flicked down the catches. Dan cleared his throat. 'What do you do for an encore?'

My cheeks were on fire but I managed to smile. 'It's your turn now.'

'If you think I'm following that then you are seriously deluded.' He nodded at the clock on the wall. 'It's lunchtime. I'll show you where to leave your flute before we go and eat.'

As we walked over to Melody House, Dan asked if I'd signed up for any of the afternoon's sporting activities.

'Not yet. I meant to ask Lucy what she was doing.'

'I'm going sailing. My boat's a solo, but you can squeeze two people in, if you're up for it?'

'Sounds like fun.'

'Is that a yes?'

'Yes,' I agreed. 'It is.'

There was a buzz of chatter coming from the dining room that paused as we entered, then restarted with a fresh intensity. I knew from the furtive, and not so furtive, glances directed my way that I was the topic of conversation. Dan looked worried and positioned himself between the diners and me as we queued for lunch. I'd been ravenous but suddenly I wasn't so hungry. I took a couple of sandwiches with fillings I didn't recognise. I loaded my plate with an apple and a carton of juice, then looked around for Lucy. A wall of faces stared back at me. The older students quickly looked away when I caught their eye but the younger kids gazed back with unbridled curiosity.

'There's Lucy,' Dan nodded to the back of the room where Lucy and Claudia were sharing an otherwise empty table. He weaved round the tables glancing back occasionally to make sure that I was following.

It was painfully clear that I was being talked about from the way the conversation trailed off, only to restart after I'd passed by. With a growing feeling of dread I put my tray down and slid into the seat next to Lucy's. Dan sat on my other side.

'What?' I asked, not really sure that I wanted to know.

'What, what?' asked Lucy, trying and failing to sound as if she genuinely hadn't a clue what I was asking her.

'Why is everyone staring at me?'

Claudia waved a half-eaten sandwich at me. 'It's nothing. Little children, that's all, spreading the rumours.'

'Rumours?' My heart pounded.

'It's no secret that you're the girl without the memory.

There was something about you on the local news. Erin McKeever's still not here. People make…' her eyes narrowed as she searched for the correct word, 'assumptions.'

'They think I'm Erin?'

Claudia shrugged. 'Maybe, but that would be good, no? At least then you find out who you are.'

'I guess so.' I bit into a sandwich and chewed mechanically. My thoughts were all over the place. I badly wanted to know who I was, but at the same time knowing scared me.

'It must be strange,' Claudia continued. 'Do you feel loneliness?'

'Amber wouldn't be the only one to be homesick,' said Dan. 'It's the first time that many of the students here have been away from their families. They soon get over it. It doesn't take long to make friends, especially when there's so much to do. Amber and I are sailing after lunch. What have you two signed up for?'

'Volleyball,' said Lucy.

'Same.' Claudia drained her drink. 'I get dessert. Who wants anything?'

'Me. The Waterside chocolate cake is to die for. Does your mum make it?' Lucy leaned over me to aim her question at Dan.

'Mum, cook?' Dan laughed. 'She's a musician. Luckily for us she's finally accepted that music is what she does best. Waterside now has a chef.'

'Your mother is very good music maker.' Claudia stood up. 'I get you a big slice of cake, Lucy.'

I finished my sandwiches and apple, then walked with Dan through the woods to the loch. A couple of instructors, wearing red polo shirts, were lifting kayaks out of a long wooden shed in preparation for the afternoon. They called out a greeting. Dan called back to them as he threaded his way between the sailing dinghies perched on wheeled frames.

'Your boats have wheels!'

'The wheels are the launching trolleys,' said Dan. 'The trolley is used to transport the boat down to the water.' A swarm of tiny winged insects buzzed around us. One landed on my arm and Dan slapped it away.

'Don't! You'll hurt it.'

'It's a mosquito.'

'And?'

Dan stared at me as if I was out of my mind. 'They bite.'

Indignation welled inside me. 'There's still no need to hurt them.'

'Mosquitos eat you alive if you let them.'

'Surely there's another way of dealing with them?' I couldn't explain why I felt so passionate about protecting the tiny biting creatures.

'You can get a repellent,' said Dan. 'Mostly I just kill them.' He laughed at my horrified expression. 'Clearly you're not from around here. The mosquito is public enemy number one.'

I shivered, not liking Dan's casual attitude to killing something just because it annoyed you.

'Cold? That's my boat there, the one with the yellow hull. Come and help me pull her down to the loch. You'll soon warm up.'

By the time we'd got the boat on the water and I'd pulled the launch trolley away from the shoreline, I was extremely hot. I'd also stopped being annoyed with Dan over the mosquitoes. There was barely enough room for two in the boat. Any embarrassment I felt at being squashed up so close to Dan disappeared as he taught me the basics of sailing. To skim across the loch, with the wind in my face and the water hissing under my feet, was sheer magic. When I took a turn at the wooden helm it was like handling a well-trained animal. The wood vibrated with excitement yet responded to my lightest touch.

'You're a natural,' Dan told me. His face was proud, as if I'd achieved something incredibly clever. I put my skill down to a lucky quirk of birth. Or was it? For all I knew I could be a keen sailor. A while later my thoughts turned to Erin McKeever. At once the pleasure and happiness I'd been feeling drained away. What was I doing out here, in the middle of a loch, having fun with a boy who in some ways felt so familiar, yet I hardly knew? I should be indoors, searching for my true identity. Erin was a definite lead. I would start with her. I faced Dan, shouting loudly to make myself heard over the noisy susurration of the water. 'Can we go back?'

Dan was surprised, but if he was disappointed he hid it well. 'Not enjoying it?' he asked.

'I love it. But there's been a lot of new stuff…' I faltered, unsure how much to confide in him.

'You've had enough.' He smiled his understanding. Pushing the tiller to the opposite side of the boat he shouted, 'About turn, mind your head.'

We both ducked as the boom swung over and the boat turned. Dan steered a zigzag course back, expertly avoiding the other sailing boats and kayaks full of giggling students. As we reached the shallows he let the sail out and raised the centreboard, instructing me to pull up the rudder. It came easily and I shot home the pin to stop it from dropping back into the water. The boat slid gently onto the shore, its hull crunching over the stones.

I jumped out to get the trolley but Dan stopped me.

'I'm staying out,' he called. He hopped out of the boat and jogged round to her bow.

I was a teensy bit disappointed. I'd half hoped he might ask where I was going and then offer to help. But it was probably better if I worked alone. Dan re-launched his boat and I couldn't help but admire his suntanned legs and straining calf muscles. He boarded, jumping neatly like a cat, and deftly reinserted the centreboard and rudder. The boat kicked, and he took control by reining in the sail. He waved as he pulled the tiller round and headed for the middle of the loch.

I waved back and my heart dipped with regret. I would have stayed out longer if it wasn't for the adrenalin coursing through me. I knew I'd find it impossible to settle until I'd found out more about Erin McKeever. Mia must have her details. I'd ask if she could ring her. Then, if no one answered the phone, I would track down her relatives, using the internet. What if I *was* Erin? An unwelcome thought crash-landed in my head. My legs felt like they were walking in stone boots and I slowed down. I covered my ears with my hands in an effort to blot out the thought. My mother. I was desperate for her to be alive. I wanted it so badly that it made me feel sick.

On I ploughed, past the boys' cabins that were just

visible through the trees. Shortly afterwards I left the meandering path to forge my own, quicker, way through the forest. There was nothing subtle about my approach. I must have sounded like a herd of *elefanta*, but at least it kept the mosquitoes away. When I arrived at the back of Melody House I circumnavigated the gardens, bordered with bushes and thick shrubs, and came out in the car park. With my goal in sight I upped the pace as I crossed over to the house.

The front door opened and Mia stepped outside, accompanied by a tiny girl with a bright mass of ginger curls. She saw me and waved for me to join her. I sighed as I went over. I'd been hoping to get her alone. On closer inspection the girl was much older than her diminished height suggested. She had a bunch of freckles that she'd tried to hide with make-up. Her eyes were highlighted with kohl and she wore shiny red lip gloss. She looked bored, as if she didn't really want to be here. I sincerely hoped that Mia didn't want me to show her around.

'This is Erin,' said Mia. 'Her mum got the dates muddled, so she's a little late arriving. Erin, this is Amber.'

'Hi,' I said. You'd never have guessed at the turmoil raging inside me. I was devastated, but at the same time weirdly relieved. All the while I didn't know the truth I could cling to the hope that my mother hadn't been with me in the car accident.

Mia touched my arm. In a low voice she asked, 'Were you looking for me, Amber? I'm giving Erin the welcome tour but I could spare you a few minutes if it's urgent?'

'No, it's fine. It was nothing important. I'll catch you later.'

'Well, if you're sure?' Mia hesitated.

'I'm sure, thanks.' I smiled brightly, then walked off in the opposite direction. I didn't feel like going back to my room. I'd spent enough time staring at walls, so I veered off the path and into the woods that ran parallel to the drive. The mixed trees were interspersed with feathery bracken and bushes adorned with brightly coloured flowers. It was beautiful, but I was barely aware of anything except for the thud of my heart as it kept time with my feet. Eventually I found my way blocked by a dense row of bushes with long, prickly leaves. I squeezed through them undeterred, my hair occasionally snagging on a branch, until I found myself in a clearing. The ground was covered with clumps of a tough-looking plant covered with small purple flowers. I sat down and sank my head on my arms. The tears came fast, hot and salty, spurting from my eyes like water from a burst pipe. I cried for ages, until I felt completely empty; then I took a deep breath and pulled myself together. With the back of my hands I wiped my face. I combed the broken twigs from my hair and pushed it back over my shoulders. Then I stood up and brushed the dirt from my clothes. Last of all, I rearranged my face. I couldn't quite manage cheerful, but as expressions go it, was a passable attempt at *I'm fine*.

SEVEN

While no two days at Waterside were identical, they soon took on a familiar pattern. My alarm woke me at seven. I'd get up straight away and nip across the corridor for a wash. Then I'd get dressed. I always performed a ten-minute stretching routine before I hitched up with Lucy, to walk over to Melody House for breakfast. The routine was something I'd put together from a book that I'd found in our common room, downstairs in Chopin. The need to exercise regularly, to keep fit and supple, was so deep-seated that I suspected it was something I'd done in my previous life. None of the exercises in the book, *New York City Ballet Workout*, were familiar. I seemed to have a near photographic memory, though, and learned them with ease.

Dan had breakfast with his parents but he often joined our group for lunch and dinner. The group consisted of Lucy, Claudia, Amy, Ellie, George and Josh. Tiny Erin, with her springy ginger curls, sometimes sat with us but mostly she preferred her own company. Claudia said she was sulking because she didn't want to be here. Her parents had forced her to come to Waterside instead of going on holiday to Tenerife with her two best friends.

It was more fun with Dan around and my mood always lifted when he arrived. Dan was friendly with everyone, but we seemed to get on especially well together. I felt like I'd always known him. I was relaxed and laughed more often when I was in his company.

After breakfast I always had a private flute lesson, followed by orchestra, and then small group ensemble. The latter changed daily as the music tutors mixed students with different instruments to see how well they played together. I loved all the sessions but I enjoyed my flute lesson best. Mr Mason was teaching me how to read sheet music, even though my memory was so good that if I heard a tune once I could play it right through.

'It's no good relying on hearing an unfamiliar piece before you can play it. A real musician must learn to decode the music from the page,' he told me.

It struck me that it would be quite helpful if there were a written guide to life. I could do with a book to help me decode some of the everyday mysteries I was up against. It still bugged me that Dan killed mosquitoes, especially when insect repellents were available. It was the needless killing of them that upset me the most. Their bite hurt, but it wasn't that bad. I would have understood if Dan had been going to eat the insects after he'd killed them, but when I mentioned that he'd roared with laughter. I'm sure he thought I was joking. To stop me dwelling on things that didn't make sense I threw myself into the challenge of learning to read music. It wasn't difficult because I really enjoyed it, and the extra work quickly paid off. Before long I could read the music for lots of tunes.

There was a downside, however, to immersing myself in so much musical activity. It left me buzzing, literally. Sometimes I'd be so wired that the mind control became a natural reflex – like breathing. I had to watch myself then, because according to the internet, moving objects by mind control, or telekinesis as it was called, wasn't normal. In fact, most scientists believed its existence hadn't been convincingly demonstrated. So what did that tell me? Nothing, really! I still didn't know if I'd always been different, or if my extrasensory skills were a result of the accident. I longed to talk about it to someone, but I wasn't sure whom I could trust. Dan came high on my list of possible confidants, but something held me back. If, as I strongly suspected, my telekinetic skills were peculiar to me alone, then it was a massive secret to burden anyone with. What if I told Dan and the knowledge was too much for him to keep to himself? He might tell Mia and Jeff. A secret shared is a secret spread. The Marshalls were lovely people, and incredibly generous, but how would they feel about me if they knew what I could do? It might frighten them, like it had the auxiliary at the hospital, and they may tell someone official, like Nicky. I didn't want to end up back in hospital, being subjected to endless tests. What if I was considered a danger? A public enemy! Would I be treated like a mosquito – and eliminated?

In the afternoons everyone played sport. I was okay at most things so I usually got picked for a team. I handled a kayak with deadly efficiency, but sailing was my real passion. It was Dan's too. He frequently took me out in his boat and I looked forward to sailing with him. We were relaxed in each other's company. Dan didn't talk incessantly, like Lucy. Don't get me wrong, she was bubbly and great fun to be with, but I craved the space Dan afforded me. Often we'd sail in silence, communicating merely with looks. Sometimes, albeit briefly, I forgot that I hadn't a clue who the real me was. I liked being Amber.

The first week flew past. It was Saturday again, the only day of the week when there weren't any music lessons. Dan and Josh, a tall gangly violinist with jet black hair and an infectious smile, planned to drive into Kirkgreen and they invited Lucy and me to join them.

'To do what?' I asked.

Lucy stared at me like I was from another world, 'To window shop, hang out together and generally have fun.'

I could think of millions of things more fun than window shopping, and there were plenty of gorgeous places to hang out here at Waterside. My own personal favourite was on the shores of the north side of the loch. Lucy, however, wanted to go to Kirkgreen and she persuaded me to go along too. Melody House had a double garage and we arranged to meet the boys there. Dan was getting the car out as we arrived, a small blue thing with four doors. Josh took the passenger seat, so Lucy and I got in the back.

'This car yours then?' asked Josh, as Dan pulled away. 'Bet the insurance was expensive.'

'It cost almost as much as the car,' Dan agreed.

Josh whistled. 'Man! I thought as much! My parents are giving me driving lessons for my birthday in December. Buying a car and running it is down to me, though.'

'I'm getting driving lessons for my birthday too,' said Lucy. 'I'll be seventeen in January. What about you, Amber?'

There was an awkward silence, then Lucy smacked her hand to her head. 'Sorry! Stupid question.'

'No problem,' I said lightly. 'The doctor wasn't sure about my age. I might be able to drive already. Want to let me have a go, Dan?'

'Tempting as that offer sounds, no.' Dan caught my eye

in the rear-view mirror and smiled at me.

When we arrived in Kirkgreen I felt exactly the same way about it as before. The streets were depressingly narrow. The tall, grey stone buildings added to the feeling that there was too much crammed into one area. It made me slightly claustrophobic. Dan navigated his way through the town and parked alongside the river. I was pleased. I felt I could breathe properly here. Josh wanted new strings for his violin and Dan had to go to the post office to send a parcel for his mum. Lucy was keen to look at clothes. We agreed to split and meet up later for coffee at the Burnside Café. I thought I'd spend my free time walking along the riverbank, but Lucy wouldn't hear of it. She linked her arm through mine and practically towed me along to the high street, to look at clothes with her. She spent an eternity going in to similar-looking shops and trying things on. To say I didn't get it was an understatement.

'Isn't this fun? Why don't you try something on, Amber?'

'I don't need anything.'

Lucy rounded on me, her eyes wide with surprise. 'A girl always needs *something*. But even if you think you don't, that's not the point. Trying stuff on is fun.'

I liked Lucy a lot and she was clearly popular with the

students at summer school. If she thought that spending a morning trying on outfits was a normal and fun thing to do, then it was good enough for me. The next shop we went into I took a handful of clothes into the changing room next to hers. We had a giggle. When I squeezed into a pair of black drainpipe jeans Lucy could hardly stand for laughing.

'Amber the Goth,' she choked out.

I filed the word in my memory so that I could look it up on the internet later. But, if I'm being honest, I still couldn't see the appeal of window shopping. I was relieved when it was time to meet the boys.

The Burnside Café looked old and uninviting but it was surprisingly welcoming once you were through the door. Its high ceilings and fresh yellow paintwork created a light airy feel. There was a variety of tables, in different shapes and sizes, with an assortment of chairs to match. Dan led us towards a low, round wooden table surrounded by squashy armchairs. My fingers informed me that the chairs were made of a synthetic fabric. This was something else I'd noticed about myself. I was brilliant at identifying materials by sight or touch. I was very careful to keep this to myself ever since Erin had called me anal when I mentioned in a conversation that her flute was made of a nickel alloy.

'What do you want to drink?' asked Dan, indicating that Josh, Lucy and I should sit down. Lucy sank into an armchair, giggling as she pitched back further than she'd expected. I remained standing. 'I'll get the drinks.'

'It's my treat.'

'You drove. The least I can do is to get some drinks,' I insisted. It was only my second time in a café that I could remember. I wanted as many new experiences as possible in the hope that something might kick-start my memory.

Dan looked obstinate and I hoped he wasn't going to argue. Surely he could see how much this meant to me? I faced him out until reluctantly he said, 'Thanks. In that case I'll have a cola.'

'Me, too,' said Josh.

'Latte for me,' said Lucy, sitting up. 'Do you want a hand?

'I can manage.' I queued up at the counter. When it was my turn I recalled the drinks order and added a cappuccino for myself. The Waterside chef made a mean cappuccino and I'd taken to drinking them at morning break. The barista slapped a tray on the counter and two saucers. While the coffees were dispensed from an industrial sized coffee machine, she poured two glasses of cola and stuck straws in them.

'Chocolate on the cappuccino?' The barista turned,

chocolate shaker in hand.

'Please.' I lifted the tray from the counter when she'd finished. The barista shot me a suspicious glare.

'That's £8.40'

'£8.40?'

'That's right.'

My cheeks burned as I suddenly realised I didn't have any money. I'd forgotten to bring my purse with me. I glanced over to our group but they weren't paying me any attention. Lucy was telling a story with much hand waving. Dan and Josh were totally enthralled. The lady behind me checked her watch and muttered something about being in a hurry.

'I'm sorry. I've forgotten my money. I'll be right back.'

'Leave the drinks here.' The barista's tone was far from friendly.

My hands trembled as I set the tray back on the counter. It felt like the substantial queue of people waiting for drinks were all staring at me as I walked over to our table. Dan saw me approach and he jumped up out of his seat.

'Amber, what's up?'

I bit my lip, wishing he would lower his voice. He was so loud and it felt like everyone in the café was staring at me. 'I don't have any money. It's back at Waterside.'

'You poor thing! How embarrassing.' Lucy immediately

reached for her bag and rummaged in it for her purse.

Josh went for his wallet, but Dan was already halfway to the counter and called back, 'I'm on it.'

A part of me wanted to find a dark corner where I could curl up into a ball. A stronger streak of pride made me follow Dan to the counter, where I deliberately made eye contact with the barista. She returned my gaze with barely concealed amusement and took the note Dan handed her. She passed back a handful of change and Dan tipped it on to the tray with the drinks.

'Thanks, I'll pay you back when we get home.' Mia had given me an allowance after our shopping trip together. Money was something that meant little to me. I couldn't get to grips with it and still had no sense of its value. Maybe I was used to getting things on account. Or maybe I stole them! It didn't help that there was nowhere to spend money at Waterside, as the summer school was all-inclusive.

'No problem.' Dan's voice, with its gentle Scottish burr, brought unexpected tears to my eyes. I blinked them back. 'Sorry about that, I didn't think.'

'Amber, stop apologising.'

'I feel so bad.' I felt especially guilty that I'd been irritated by Dan's loudness.

'It's fine, really. You can make it up to me another

time, if you insist.'

'I do.'

'Right, I'll keep you to that,' Dan winked, and my heart skipped.

I sipped my coffee slowly. The conversation flowed over me as I contemplated what had happened. Maybe staying at a summer school wasn't a good idea. It was a pretty unique experience. It might explain why, over a week on from my accident, I couldn't remember anything about my old life. It felt like my memory was playing a game with me. Games were good. I was getting a reputation for my competitiveness, especially at basketball. But the thing I liked most about games was they had rules. Unlike the game my memory was playing, which had come without them.

EIGHT

On Sunday morning a meeting was held for all students to discuss the forthcoming mini-concert on Friday. Although the concert was less formal than the end-of-summer one we were urged to give our best, as there would be a sizeable audience of parents. The solo parts were assigned. Dan, Josh, Lucy and I were asked if we would perform as a quartet. We agreed and were given music for a compilation of tunes that were regularly played at the last night of an annual series of concerts called the Proms.

I glanced at the music as we made our way to a music room, in the Margaret Becker building, for our first practice. 'What's the Proms? Why is the same music always played on the last night?'

'Seriously?' asked Josh. 'Man, what universe are you from?'

His expression of disbelief made me laugh. 'Not this one,' I teased him back.

'The Proms are arguably the most prestigious classical music events in the whole world. They're held at the Royal Albert Hall in London. It's every musician's dream to play at the Proms.'

'Well, maybe I already have played there,' I said, smiling.

'Amber, the way you play the flute, nothing would surprise me,' said Josh.

We collected our instruments from the cupboard, then crowded into a practice room. We played scales and a few simple tunes to warm up. Then Dan suggested everyone should read through the music. The melodies were fun to play and everyone was impressed with how quickly I'd learned to read the notation.

'Mr Mason says I've made such fast progress because I'm not learning to read music from scratch. He thinks the knowledge is there, it's just buried away in my subconscious,' I stressed, not wanting to be the geek.

At first, as we ran through the tunes, we made several mistakes. It didn't lessen our enjoyment at playing together, especially the last piece, a jaunty number called the 'Sailor's Hornpipe'. Josh knew the words, something along the lines of what to do with a drunken sailor. He sang along as he played his violin. I loved making music on the flute. My head was spinning when we finished our repertoire. High on the music, I spun my flute into the air by telekinesis. Time slowed as I realised my mistake. All eyes were suddenly fixed on my instrument, twirling as gracefully as a pirouetting ballerina, directly above my head. I let go of the mind control. The flute plummeted. I caught it just before it hit the floor. Dan's face was a moving picture of amazement, horror and then relief.

'Man, did you just throw that?' asked Josh.

'N-n-no,' I stammered. 'I was going to put it on the table but I tripped.'

'Great catch! That's why she's popular in basketball.' Lucy sounded slightly out of breath.

Sweat beaded in my hairline. My hands shook so violently that I had to put the flute on the table before I really did drop it.

'Good thing Mum wasn't here to see that! She might reconsider her loan.'

Dan was joking, I think. I returned his smile with a somewhat shakier one.

Josh snatched up his bow. He launched into a rendition of the 'Sailor's Hornpipe' and sang along with the words, 'What shall we do with the drunken Amber?'

It was impossible not to laugh, even though it wasn't funny. I couldn't remember if I'd ever been drunk, but the music left me light-headed and with hardly any control over my telekinetic sense. I had to do something about it. It would have been disastrous if I'd damaged Mia's flute, but to expose my *special* talent would be catastrophic.

'That's enough,' Lucy punched Josh playfully on the

arm. Obediently he stopped singing and laid his violin back in its case. He rounded on her and tickled her until she begged him to stop.

Dan's eyes met mine and I saw something resembling disappointment. He suspected that I'd lied. Maybe he'd seen me throw the flute. He definitely wasn't convinced that I'd stumbled. I wished that I could tell him what had happened. I wasn't a careless person. If anything I was over-obsessive with the care I took with other people's things.

When Lucy and Josh stopped messing around we ran through the tunes one more time. My performance was flawed. I was far too worried that I'd lose control again to give myself fully to the music and I played like a beginner.

'It'll get better,' Dan assured me. We left the room ahead of Lucy and Josh, who were having a sword fight with a couple of drumsticks. I hoped he was right. I couldn't afford to make mistakes, especially ones that would get me noticed in front of an audience.

The more I worried about suppressing my telekinetic skills, the harder my fight to control them became. By midweek I was shattered. On Wednesday morning it was a struggle to get out of bed. It was an even bigger effort to perform my ballet exercises. All I wanted to do was to collapse in a comfy chair with a mug of strong coffee.

I stood in the middle of the room and took a deep breath. The first few moves were a killer. Once I got going I felt better, and I enjoyed stretching my muscles, as I pushed my body into positions it didn't normally assume. Exercise had definitely played a part in my previous life. My body was too supple and toned for my new regime to have been responsible for it. I held my stomach in as I began to perform a series of arabesque raises, an exercise that involved the bending of one leg while lifting the other. As I completed the balance a thought dropped into my head.

What if my telekinetic powers needed a workout? A shiver raced down my spine. The idea wasn't as mad as it sounded. Exercising my muscles gave me greater control over them, so why not my mind? I lowered my leg to the floor and sat on the bed while I thought about it. There was a risk of course. Exercising might make the telekinesis stronger and even harder to control. But it had to be worth a try. I was heading for a disaster if I didn't do something soon. I jumped up. My hands trembled and I concentrated on breathing slowly and deeply until I felt calmer. My room was on the first floor but I shut the curtains, to stop anyone who might be lurking outside from seeing me. I also shoved a chair under the door handle. I couldn't help my paranoia. I wanted to know why I was so different to everyone else before I started advertising it. When I was satisfied that the room was completely secure I looked around for something to move. Not only am I minimalist but I'm a neat freak. The possessions I'd left out were few and tidily arranged. There was only one thing for it; I'd have to mess things up. Believe it or not, going against my inbuilt tidiness was incredibly hard, but once I was over that hurdle the telekinesis was child's play. It was fun too. As I used my mind to pull open drawers and toss their contents on the floor, it made me realise that I'd been suppressing a part of me that was as natural as breathing. Better still my theory worked. I practised my mental workout daily and as the week progressed I found that I had much more control of my telekinetic skills. The music still left me buzzing, only now there was less danger that I'd lose control of my mind and accidentally reveal my weird secret.

'Amber, are you in there? I'm having a tights disaster.'

'Come in,' I said absently. I stared at my reflection in the mirror. I was having problems too. My latest attempt to put my hair up consisted of a fat chestnut bun, with unruly wisps of hair that trailed down my face like ivy on a wall. My black eye was almost gone; all that remained was a deep purple smudge beneath it.

Lucy flounced into the room. Her behaviour was

so uncharacteristic that I temporarily forgot about my problematic hair.

'What's up?' I asked.

'I bought really expensive tights for tonight. Then I snagged them. The ladder runs right the way up my leg. I thought the pack had two pairs but it doesn't. Now I'm without tights. Please tell me that you have a spare pair I can borrow.'

'In the top drawer, with the socks.'

With exaggerated care Lucy pulled a pair of black tights from the drawer. 'Amber you're a star. I hate getting ready for concerts. Once I'm there, in my seat, I'm fine. The adrenalin kicks in and stops me from feeling so nervous. But until then I'm a wreck.'

'I'm nervous too.' I didn't add that it was for a different reason. I wasn't so concerned about how I played, more who I was playing to. I clearly came from a musical background. What if someone in the audience recognised me?

'Looks like you need some help with your hair.' Lucy came and stood behind me.

I pulled out the blue hair tie that was securing my bun and the hair tumbled down my back. 'I hate these things,' I complained. I threw the tie across the dressing table. 'They're so unflattering.'

I didn't get the whole uniform thing. Why did the orchestra have to dress identically? The girls had to wear black skirts and white open-neck blouses and have their hair fastened with a blue tie. The boys wore black trousers and matching jacket, a white short-sleeved shirt and a blue necktie. Everyone was made to have black shoes. We looked like the giant-sized chess pieces on the draughtboard in the outdoor play area. We also looked like soldiers! I shuddered. That was my problem. Uniform was for soldiers, not musicians.

Lucy scooped my hair up in her hands and started brushing it. 'Hmm, it's too long and thick for a bun. Let's try something else. Her fingers flew round my head as she deftly caught up strands of hair and wove it into something amazing. She secured the end with the blue hair tie and stood back to admire her efforts.

'Wow!' I turned my head sideways and squinted in the mirror to see the back. My hair looked like two long intertwined springs. 'It's so pretty. I love it. What's it called?'

'A fishtail plait. I sleep in one sometimes. Try it. You'll wake up with very curly hair.'

I arranged the fishtail plait over my shoulder. My rich brown hair perfectly complemented my necklace. The amber stone rested in the dip of my neck above my collarbone. I stroked it, then traced my fingers along the zigzag of gold supporting the stone. I'd love to know how I came by the necklace. It seemed far too special to be something that I'd bought for myself.

'You need matching earrings,' said Lucy.

I grabbed the lobes of my ears. 'I don't have my ears pierced.'

'You should get them done next time we go to Kirkgreen.'

'Maybe. Thanks for doing my hair. It looks fantastic.'

'I'd better do mine.' Lucy checked her watch. 'We're running out of time. Meet you downstairs in ten minutes.'

As Lucy and I entered the Bluewater Concert Hall, the noise deafened me. Half of the orchestra were warming up; the other half chatted. We exchanged nervous grins with Claudia, Amy, Ellie and George, who were already seated. Our chairs, assigned in the rehearsals, were near the front. At first, I'd been disappointed that we weren't playing in Margaret Becker, on the stunning outdoor stage. Margaret Becker, it seemed, was kept for more prestigious events, like the end-of-summer school concert. When I reached my seat I stood with my back to the orchestra and looked around. Bluewater was a beautiful concert hall too. The fresh cream and fawn walls made the room feel light and spacious. A graceful cut glass chandelier hung from the middle of the room. It cast tiny rainbows on the ceiling. The audience seats were tiered and upholstered in rich blue velour.

When I sat down, my skirt rose up high over my knees. The skirt was a style that Lucy called pencil and was tight and unyielding as I tugged it down. Lucy was having a similar battle with her skirt and we shared a sympathetic smile. I was preoccupied with getting comfortable and I almost missed the boys coming in. I glanced up just in time and saw Dan and Josh pause in the doorway, before they made their entrance. Dan looked uncharacteristically ill at ease. He gripped his sax case as if it was an offensive weapon. His show of nerves surprised me. For a second I was disorientated. It felt like I'd been expecting to see someone else, with far greater poise and sophistication than Dan, and I was slightly disappointed. Dan's nerves reminded me how little I knew about him. His smart clothes made him seem even more of a stranger. His broad chest strained against the confines of his crisp black jacket and his legs seemed longer in tailored trousers. His unruly blonde hair lay neatly and his face, tanned from his outdoor lifestyle, made his shirt look whiter than swan's feathers. My breath caught in my throat. No matter how nervous Dan looked, no matter how uncharacteristically Dan, he was still gorgeous.

'Wow!' said Lucy huskily. 'Josh scrubs up well.'

I dragged my eyes away from Dan to admire Josh. He was taller than Dan and thin as a boat hook. The outline of his bony shoulders reminded me of a coat hanger, displaying a smart new jacket. He wore the jacket open. A blue Waterside tie snaked down his shirt and disappeared under the waistband of his trousers. His black hair was pushed to one side, so for once you could see his eyes. Agreed, he was smart and handsome but he didn't make my pulse race the way Dan had. I wasn't the only girl to admire Dan as he took to his seat. He didn't seem to notice. His eyes were on me. They widened as he gave me a long, appraising stare. 'You look amazing.'

I suddenly felt hot. 'So do you,' I croaked back.

We drank each other in, wordlessly. I knew it was going to take all my powers of concentration to focus on the music tonight. Dan broke eye contact first, becoming brisk and businesslike as he lifted his saxophone out off its case. I slotted together Mia's flute and licked my lips as I prepared to warm up. I'd only managed a few scales when our conductor, Peter Lassiter, took up his position at the front of the orchestra and tapped the music stand to get our attention. Things became a little hazy after that. There was a brief rehearsal before the audience was seated. The lights dimmed. A magical hush stole around the room. In that short moment of absolute silence the air was heavy with expectation. Then the orchestra burst to life and sent the opening bars of Handel's 'Arrival of the Queen of Sheba' soaring up to the roof. The music lifted me and stole away my nerves. Who cared if anyone in the audience recognised me? I'd deal with it later. My fingers flew along the keys making music sweeter than a lark's song.

I thought the orchestra played the opening tune brilliantly. As the last note died away the audience erupted and clapped passionately. It was so unexpected that I didn't have time to control the terror that slammed me. My whole body shook. Mia's flute slid through my fingers, but frightened as I was I had enough sense to try to save it. With a light touch of mind control, I was able to slow its fall and catch it. I was pretty certain that no one had seen me. I laid the flute safely across my lap. Dan reached out and covered my hand with his. 'Are you all right?' he asked.

'Yes. There's no damage to the flute.'

'Forget the flute. What happened just then? You looked like you were freaking out.'

I stared around the concert hall. The clapping was fading and I could hear the rustle of music as the orchestra prepared for their next piece.

'The clapping,' I faltered, not sure how to explain my reaction to it.

'The applause made you jump?'

Yes, it was... unexpected.' It was more than that though. The noise had frightened me. It felt like a warning of something untoward.

Dan gave a low chuckle. 'The audience is mostly parents. You could hiccup and they'd clap.'

'Really?' Hiccupping would evoke that response too?

Dan gave a loud laugh and earned one of Peter's infamous glares. He squeezed my hand and whispered, 'Not really, but you get my drift. Be prepared for lots of clapping. They'll applaud after every piece.'

'Right,' I said weakly. Thoughts sped through my head faster than the traffic on the Kirkgreen bypass. It was a natural assumption that I came from a musical background. It was a safe guess that I'd played in many concerts. Why had the applause upset me so badly then? A memory flickered deep in my mind. As I went to dive after it, Dan dropped my hand. 'Ready?' he whispered.

Around me the orchestra sat, instruments poised, as they watched Peter's fluttering hands. I lifted my flute and the memory slid out of reach.

NINE

The concert was a huge success. The applause went on for ages and we played two encores. Afterwards, there was a reception for the musicians and the audience in the function room. Mia and Jeff sought me out.

'You played so well,' said Mia, hugging me.

'Like a maestro,' Jeff agreed. He patted me on the shoulder.

I felt myself blush. 'We're all maestros here. It must be the brilliant music teachers.'

'Yes, but you did especially well considering your circumstances,' said Mia. Her voice shook as she added, 'We're proud of you, aren't we, Jeff?'

'Definitely.'

'Thanks.' I was feeling emotional too. Mia and Jeff were so kind. I had been lucky when fate threw me in their path.

'Go and have a drink to celebrate,' said Mia. 'There's champagne for our older students.'

She beckoned to one of the waitresses and swiped a tall glass from her tray. She handed it to me before disappearing in a crowd of parents who wanted to congratulate her on the success of the concert. I sipped at the pale sparkling liquid. It was delicious, although the bubbles made my nose wrinkle. A waiter, carrying a silver tray, offered me a canapé. I took it, and as I bit into it was suddenly overcome with tiredness. I was ready for bed. I looked around for Dan, to say goodnight before I left. I spotted him eventually, on the opposite side of the room. He was chatting to the guests while he helped to hand around drinks. I watched him closely but each time he moved on from a parent someone else claimed him. Clearly he was well known and popular. It was ages before we managed to exchange a few brief words, as I returned my empty glass and he refilled his tray from the small bar.

'Sorry about this, but my parents expect it. It's all part and parcel of running a successful music school.'

'That's all right. You seem to know a lot of people.' I hid my disappointment that he couldn't spend more time with me.

'A lot of our students are local. They attend courses here throughout the year. And the ones who aren't local keep on coming back for the residential courses.'

'I'm not surprised. It's a fantastic place.'

'Thanks. Look, I should get back, but tomorrow's Saturday; there are no music lessons. How about we go sailing in the morning?'

'I'd like that.'

'Good.' Dan smiled and something inside me melted. 'Meet you at nine then, at the boat.'

He was gone before I had time to reply.

'Hey!' Lucy snagged me as I drifted past and drew me into a conversation with her and Josh. I chatted with them for a bit then, smothering a yawn, I said goodnight.

'Amber!' I had almost got through the door when Claudia bore down on me. She had a silver tray, piled high with assorted goodies. In her wake trailed Amy, Ellie, George and several other older, students. Everyone carried food and drinks on trays. 'We have the party down by the loch. Come with us.'

'It sounds fun, but I'm really tired. I'm going to bed.'

Claudia's face fell. 'But this is my last night. My parents are here. Tomorrow we must travel for two weeks around Scotland. Then we go back to Germany.'

I didn't feel like partying down by the loch, but I could hardly say no when it was my last chance to spend some time with Claudia. I liked her direct, no-nonsense manner and would miss having her around. With an effort, I pulled myself together and said, 'In that case, how could I refuse!'

'Good,' she replied. 'You will enjoy it.'

To my surprise I loved the impromptu loch-side party. I soon forgot how tired I was and stayed up much later than

I'd meant to. I crawled into bed a little after midnight. I fell asleep immediately and began to dream.

I had to find Dan. There was something important that I needed to tell him. He was supposed to be practising a sax solo, but he wasn't in any of the music rooms. I ran through Bluewater and then the Margaret Becker building. As I went I called out to the students and staff and asked if anyone knew where Dan was. No one did.

'Dan, where are you?' My news was so big that it couldn't wait.

'Dan?' My feet left the ground. Now I was flying, skimming across the treetops like a kestrel in search of a tiny mouse. A long while later I found Dan, alone near the boathouse. He was patching a sail on his boat. I dived to the ground and landed a short distance from him. Dan looked up. He waved at me, but as I approached he took off. He skipped down to the edge of the loch with exaggerated steps. It would have been funny if my message hadn't been urgent. Instead, I felt panicked and cross as Dan pranced along the banks of the loch, with his knees bobbing up and down. I called out. I needed him to understand how important my message was, but my voice wouldn't work properly. It sounded like the whine of a mosquito. As my frustration rose I was seized with a powerful surge of dream energy. Half running, half flying, I finally reached him and tapped him on the shoulder. He swung round and skipped on the spot with gigantic steps. I

was so out of breath that at first I couldn't speak. Dan's blue eyes twinkled mischievously. He doubled up with laughter as I tried and failed to choke out my message. At last Dan stopped skipping. He wrapped his arms around me and pulled me close. For a long minute he stared at me intently, then he bowed his head until our mouths were almost touching. I could feel his breath, warm on my face, and the beat of his heart through his cotton shirt. 'Amber,' he whispered, 'I've wanted this for ages.' He held me tight and kissed me.

His soft lips sent delicious shivers racing down my spine. I pressed against him, weaving my fingers into his blonde curls. Dan explored the inside of my mouth with the tip of his tongue and I melted. I closed my eyes and wished that the kiss would never end. When he finally drew away I kept my arms around his waist as I stared up at him. He held my gaze and that's when I realised that something wasn't right. His eyes were much bluer than those I remembered, the lashes framing them were longer and thicker. His face seemed different too. I raised my hand to his cheek. It was fuller, with higher cheekbones and a slimmer nose. Confusion filled me. This wasn't Dan. I'd been kissing a complete stranger! I twisted away but the boy pulled me back and kissed me firmly on the mouth. It felt so right. The world could end and I wouldn't care. It was as if I'd finally come home. I wanted to stay here in the arms of this boy whose lips left me burning with desire. He wanted me too. He pressed his nose to mine and murmured my *name, my real name. He repeated it over and over again. We clung together and I drowned in his kisses.*

I woke with a start. My heart raced and my lips were swollen. I pressed my hand to them. The cold touch of my fingertips slowly eased their longing. The room was in semi-darkness, morning still on her way, but I couldn't get back to sleep. I lay curled in a ball as I relived my dream. I didn't want to let it go but, like snow in rain, the pictures melted. My bed was hot and lumpy. I got up, washed and dressed. I did my exercises, doubling my efforts, to erase the ache of desire. It didn't work. I decided I needed a mug of hot, strong coffee.

Lucy was sleeping in but Claudia was up early, to be ready for when her parents came to collect her. We ate breakfast together. There were only a few other students in the dining hall. Most people were still in bed, recovering from the concert.

'Why are you up so early?' Claudia slathered strawberry jam on a warm croissant.

'I'm going sailing with Dan.'

'Ah!' she gave me a knowing look. 'You like each other.'

'We're very good friends.'

'Soon, you will be more than friends.'

'No!' I protested. Colour rushed to my face. Did I want more from Dan than friendship? I might, but I wasn't sure. It wasn't fair to start a relationship when my life was so full of questions. What if I was involved in something illegal? Much as I was determined to put a life of crime behind me, I would still be accountable for past misdemeanours. If I'd been very bad I might end up in a juvenile prison. My dream had been a warning. I was sure of it. My subconscious was reminding me that until I'd dealt with my past I wasn't free to start anything new.

Claudia finished chewing, then swallowed. 'We'll see.'

After breakfast, I took the woodland path to the loch. Early morning was by far my favourite time of the day; I loved the sharp nip of the fresh, new air. The sun followed me through the trees, spilling pools of gold onto the earthy ground. I breathed deeply and savoured the tangy smell of the pine and the subtle scents of the oak, birch and juniper trees. A feathered choir, hidden in the leafy canopy, sang out tunefully. I joined in, humming music from the concert.

Dan beat me to the boat. He was ready to launch it when I arrived. We exchanged greetings; then I lapsed into an awkward silence as I remembered my dream. It was stupid. Dan knew nothing about my handsome dream boy. He'd no idea how much I'd enjoyed his kiss or how the memory of him was still strong in my mind. I kept my head down and hoped that my blushing cheeks wouldn't give away such treacherous thoughts. We wheeled the boat to the water's edge and took off our trainers to paddle it into the icy water. The boat floated off the trolley and I jumped in to secure the tiller and rudder. Dan took the trolley back to the shore then waded after me. We hoisted the sail. A gust of wind caught it and we were off, sailing towards the middle of the loch.

We sailed in silence, squeezed up on the same side of the boat. I closed my eyes because the wind was making them water.

'Tired?' Dan asked.

'A little.'

'You played like a professional.'

'So did you. Your sax solo was amazing.'

'You didn't notice when I dropped a note?'

I opened my eyes. Dan was looking at me so intently that it made me smile. He'd got me there and he knew it.

'Maybe, but it was only a little mistake.'

'I was nervous,' he confessed. 'Playing in public's not really my thing.'

'Oh?' That surprised me. It was obvious that Dan had been nervous at the start of the concert. I had been too. Once we'd started playing though, I lost all my inhibitions. The music carried me to another plane and I'd assumed it would be the same for Dan.

'I love music but it's not the most important thing in my life,' he said, breaking into my thoughts. 'One day I'm going to sail around the world.'

'Really!' I was definitely up for an adventure that big. Maybe I'd sail around the world too.

'I used to go sea sailing with my grandad. He had a small yacht. He lived in the south in a place called Bournemouth. It's a seaside town. Mum and Dad would put me on the overnight sleeper train and Grandad would pick me up from the station. We used to sail along to the Scilly Isles, and once we went over to France.' Dan paused, staring across the water, a faraway look in his eyes. A duck flew overhead. It skimmed across our bows, quacking loudly, and splash-landed half a metre ahead of us. 'Then Grandad got ill. He had leukaemia. He died earlier this year.'

'I'm sorry.' I wasn't sure that he'd heard me over the hiss of the water, as it rushed past the boat, until he said softly, 'Me too. I miss him so much.'

A knife twisted in my stomach, for Dan and for the grandfather who'd meant so much to him. It reminded me of the woman who'd been with me at the time of the car accident. Should I be grieving for her? Could that explain why my memory was in lockdown? Grief was a powerful thing. Forgetting my past might be a way of dealing with it.

We sailed in silence, wrapped up in our own thoughts. A long time later Dan looped a strand of my hair over his finger. 'This is fantastic.'

'Thanks,' I said shyly. I'd slept in my fishtail plait. As Lucy had promised, my hair was now a thick mass of curls. 'When are you going to sail around the world?'

'Not for ages yet, Mum and Dad want me to go to university to study for a degree in business studies, so that one day I can take over here. Edinburgh Uni is a family tradition. It's where my parents met, and where Grandad studied. He was an engineer.' From the wistful note in Dan's voice it didn't take a genius to work out that something was wrong.

'But you don't want to?'

We were approaching the shore. Dan sat up straight and pushed the tiller away from him. 'About turn.'

I ducked, as the boom swung over, and shifted my weight to balance the boat when it changed direction. In my new position I was suddenly conscious of Dan's knee pressed up close against mine. We were both wearing shorts and the soft blonde hairs on his bare legs tickled me. My chest tightened and I moved my foot slightly to break the contact.

'No, I guess not. There's a degree in architecture I'd like to do at Plymouth Uni. I haven't told Mum and Dad yet.'

'Oh.' Not very helpful, but I didn't know what else to say. 'Won't they be pleased for you?'

'Yes, they will, but they'll be disappointed too – even though they won't admit it. I'm their only child. Waterside will be mine one day.'

I stared into the loch and was mesmerised by the depth of its colour. It was like a prism; it absorbed the sun's light and split it into every shade of blue.

Dan lightly touched my arm. 'You won't tell anyone what I just said?'

'Never!' At that moment I felt very close to Dan. He'd become my best friend, someone to share my secrets with. I wanted to tell him about the flashbacks and how each time I touched my phone I experienced the same vague sense of urgency. I wondered what he'd think of my theory that I was part of something secret and dangerous. I even wanted to confess to him that I had weird telekinetic skills.

The silence weighed between us. I clenched my hands into fists and steeled myself to tell Dan everything. But as I drew breath, the voice, absent for so long, was back in my head. It rang out, shriller than a fire alarm.

NEVER tell them your real name.

I jumped and bit my lip. There was blood in my mouth

and its coppery taste made my nose wrinkle as I swallowed.

Who are you? What do you want?

But the woman with the cold voice and steely eyes disappeared without an answer.

Dan and I spent the whole morning on the loch and only came in for lunch because we were starving hungry. Side by side, we hauled the boat up onto the shore, rolled the sail round the boom and tidied the ropes. My clothes were wet and I needed to change. Dan walked with me to my cabin. As we said goodbye the front door opened and a girl I recognised strolled out. My pulse quickened as I tried to place her. She was my height, with long hair that fell over her shoulders in a honey gold wave. She had blue eyes and an air of sophistication. A red halter-top accentuated her curvy figure and her teeny shorts made her tanned legs seem very long.

'Hi,' I said, self-consciously pushing a strand of wet hair back from my face. 'Don't I know you?'

'Hardly.' The girl gave me a withering look. Then she noticed Dan and her voice immediately softened. 'Wait a minute. I'm an auxiliary at Rowan Bank Hospital. Were you a patient there? Didn't I bring you a drink? I'm Holly, Holly Jenkins.'

Was it my imagination or was there hate in Holly's eyes

as she shot me a smile?

I opened my mouth to reply and felt stupid when I had to clear my throat first.

'Of course! I'm Amber. That's a coincidence, seeing you here I mean.'

'*Weird*,' Holly smiled back and we both knew she wasn't talking about coincidences. 'What instrument do you play?'

'Flute,' I said.

'Me too and your... er... friend?'

'Dan Marshall. Sax. Welcome to Waterside, Holly.'

'Thanks Dan,' Holly turned to give him her full attention. She fluttered her eyelashes as she said, 'Can you show me the way to Melody House? I've had the tour but I'm lost already and I'd hate to miss lunch.'

'Of course, I'm headed there myself so I can take you the whole way. See you later, Amber.'

'Bye, then.' I waved as Dan and Holly left together. Not that Dan noticed. His eyes were fixed on Holly as she sashayed alongside him.

My heart fell to the pit of my stomach and, as if my feelings of inadequacy weren't enough, something else tugged at me. It was so unfamiliar that I was almost at my room before I worked it out. It was jealousy.

TEN

'Amber, catch.'

I looked up to see a basketball spinning towards me. How was I supposed to catch it? I had my hands full. I was carrying a net of balls and a set of bibs, marked with each player's position.

'I'll get it.' Lucy leapt in front of me. She caught the ball before it smacked me in the face. 'Lousy shot, Holly.'

'Sorry! I didn't realise you had your arms full.' There wasn't one drop of sincerity in Holly's voice.

'What *is* her problem?' muttered Lucy. 'She's been a cow to you ever since she started here.'

'You noticed?'

'You'd have to be blind and deaf not to. She never stops, unless Dan's around.' Lucy raised her eyebrows meaningfully.

We'd just finished a game of basketball and, by rights, it should be Lucy who was mad at me. Holly and I were on the same side and we'd buried Lucy's team by a resounding thirty-six baskets to eight. But this had nothing to do with basketball; Holly had been testing me ever since she'd arrived at Waterside. When she wasn't making bitchy comments about my fashion sense or, more specifically, my lack of it, she was asking the impossible of me. She'd pass me things when I had my hands full, or unexpectedly move obstacles into my path. I had a feeling that she was trying to catch me out. She wanted me to use my special skills, and once or twice I nearly had. The telekinesis was second nature. I had it more under control, but there were still occasions when it acted on reflex.

'Dan's not interested in her. Anyone can see he only has eyes for you,' Lucy continued.

'What?'

We reached the PE store and I dumped the basketballs on the floor while Lucy opened the door. My pulse quickened and I suddenly felt very hot.

'It's obvious. Don't tell me you haven't noticed?' Lucy stared at me in disbelief.

'It's… he's… Dan and I, we're just good friends,' I said firmly. 'We've lots of things in common.'

I busied myself with putting the basketballs away so that Lucy wouldn't see the flush of red creeping up my neck. First Claudia and now Lucy! Had anyone else noticed how well Dan and I were getting on together? How awkward. It wasn't fair of me to give Dan the impression that we could be anything more than close friends. There were too many question marks hanging over my past. I needed answers before I could get involved with him.

'Yeah, right! Josh and I are *very good friends* too. We're going to keep seeing each other by the way. He lives in Manchester. It's not that far from here. He's invited me to stay with him for a weekend in the autumn.'

'Lucy, that's great!' Lucy and Josh spent practically all their free time together. It was obvious they were keen on each other.

We came out of the shed and joined the throng of students as they crossed the field back to their cabins. Holly was walking with Erin. They looked odd together. Holly, tall and glamorous, dressed in a tight top and tiny shorts, strode out confidently, while little Erin, with her mass of ginger curls, tagged along by her side. Erin kept glancing up at Holly, like a puppy that worships its owner. And to think I'd wanted to be Erin McKeever!

'Josh and I are meeting up for a swim in the loch before dinner. Want to join us?' asked Lucy.

'Thanks, but I'm all sweaty. I'd better have a shower. I've got to see Mia later. She wants to go over some music with me for the end-of-summer concert. She's asked me to play a solo.'

Originally, Mia had asked me to perform the song that I'd first played for her and Lucy at the end-of-summer concert. She couldn't stop humming it. She said it would be a fantastic piece to include in the programme if I was still here!

The love song played constantly in my mind too. It haunted and teased me in equal measures. Its name was on the edge of my tongue yet just out of reach. It felt special. I didn't want to share it, so I pretended to Mia that I couldn't always remember how to play it. Her disappointment made me feel awful, but not enough to change my mind.

Holly sniffed delicately. 'Good idea! You really ought to get a deodorant. I can recommend a good one.'

Erin laughed and her ginger curls bounced on her shoulders.

'She wasn't talking to you, dumbo.' Lucy flapped her hands by her ears. I smiled. Holly's comments had long stopped hurting me and I'd learned that, unless I wanted to prolong an argument, it was best to ignore them.

We crossed over the drive and stopped in front of Melody House.

'Are you going back to your room?'

'Nah. My costume's in here.' Lucy patted the bag slung from her shoulder. 'You know where we are if you change your mind.'

'Thanks,' I waved as she walked away along the tree-lined path that led to the swimming jetty. When I turned back Dan was coming out of the house. He grinned and my heart did a double beat. He started to come towards me but Holly appeared and intercepted him.

'Hi there,' she called in an over loud voice. 'How about that trip in your sailing boat like you promised? I'm free now or we could fix another date for it?'

What? Dan had promised Holly a trip in his boat? But... no, I didn't want to think about it. I hastily buried the memories of being squeezed up with Dan in his boat, flying across the loch with the wind in our faces. Why shouldn't Dan go sailing with Holly? It was nothing to do with me. I didn't wait to hear his answer but started along the path to my cabin. My stomach felt heavy. I covered it with my hand and tried to press the hurt away. It was stupid to feel like this. It wasn't as if I could have gone sailing with Dan, anyway. I had an appointment to see Mia.

Nice one, Amber! Keep telling yourself that and you might even believe it. I entered Chopin and stomped up the stairs. The hall was deserted as I kicked open my bedroom door. I quickly grabbed a towel, my wash bag and some clean clothes, then I marched across the corridor to the bathroom. I showered until my skin tingled. As I reached outside the cubicle for my towel, a blast of cool air rushed in. A sudden longing for home and a people drier engulfed me.

Home – I almost had it. But, like cats in the night, the memory slipped away. I rubbed my body vigorously with the towel as if I could scrub away the frustration building inside me. When I was dressed I opened the bathroom window to blow the condensation away. I gathered up my dirty clothes and went back to my room. The door was ajar. I stopped dead. I'd definitely closed it. Deep inside me something clicked into place. I found myself running through a mental checklist with the speed and efficiency of a computer.

First rule, assess.

I leaned forward to listen. A soft rustle came from inside my room. By fine-tuning my senses I detected breathing, short and rapid. The intruder was nervous. I put my wash things on the floor and silently ticked off rule number two.

Hands free! Don't carry unnecessary baggage.

Surprise is deadly.

That was rule three. On the balls of my feet, I crept to the door. I edged round it and surveyed the room.

The intruder was Holly Jenkins. No real surprise there, then. I was treated to the sight of her long, sun-browned legs as she bent over to search the bottom drawer of my chest. I would have taken her, but rule four stopped me from doing something I might have regretted.

Words not weapons!

'Hi Holly, can I help you to find what you're looking for?'

Holly stood up and wheeled round so fast that she caught the back of her heel on the open drawer. She winced and I saw hatred flit across her face as she stared back at me.

'I... er, came to give you this music.' She reached behind and grabbed at a wodge of paper balanced on the top of my chest.

As she handed the paper to me I kept my hands firmly by my sides. 'So what are you looking for in my drawers?'

Holly didn't hesitate. She even looked me straight in the eye as she replied, 'The "Morning Mood" score. Mia asked Dan to give you this in return for it; she needs it for another student. He was on his way to see you when he ran into me and...' Holly paused and a sly smile played on her lips. 'Well, let's just say he got a little distracted. He ended up running late. I was coming here anyway and I offered to do the swap for him. I was just looking for the music.'

She thrust the paper at me again, then dropped it on the bed when I made no move to take it. I was blocking the doorway. Holly drew herself up and said coolly,

'Excuse me, I'm running late too so I'd best get going.'

You had to admire her nerve. 'What about the mobile?'

'Sorry?'

'Does Dan need his mobile phone back too?'

'Oh you mean this?' She plucked the mobile phone out of her shorts pocket. 'Is it Dan's? I thought it was yours.' A pink flush spread from Holly's hairline to her face. 'I remembered there being a fuss about your mobile at the hospital. One of the doctors was asking around for phone chargers to see if he could get your phone working again. I brought mine in, but you'd left by then, so I thought I'd try it now. Once you get your phone working it should be easy enough to find out your identity. Although I have to say, that with your talents, I'm surprised...' Holly paused significantly. She shrugged and added, 'But why would you fake memory loss?'

She tossed the mobile phone onto the bed, shouldered past me and shot off down the corridor. I couldn't stop shaking. How dare Holly sneak into my room and go through my things. I had a sudden desire to take all my clothes to the laundry and wash everything. It was lucky that I kept my own mobile on me all the time. I patted my pocket and was reassured to feel it there. It would be just typical if Holly had taken it, somehow got it to work and spilled all my secrets. I wasn't sure if I hated

Holly or feared her. I wished fervently that she'd leave me alone and let me work things out for myself. I felt like she was forcing me to face up to a past that I wasn't completely ready to confront. The checklist that I'd run through when I'd first realised there was an intruder in my room was somewhat... *professional*. Who, exactly, was I? And more to the point, what the hell was I up to? You could put Holly's actions down to sheer curiosity. But what would you say about mine?

It weighed heavily on me that Dan had shared his secrets with me but I hadn't shared mine back. I justified my secrecy by telling myself that I needed more information about my past before I confessed to anything, especially the weird flashes of memory I kept getting. I was convinced that the flashbacks were of actual events. My recent dream also furthered my conviction that my past was a lot darker than my life now. It had to be a subconscious warning. I wasn't free to get involved with Dan. Over the next couple of days I avoided being alone with him. It wasn't difficult. Lucy, Josh, Dan and I spent lots of time together as a group, rehearsing for the big end-of-summer concert, now less than three weeks away.

On Wednesday morning I woke a little after sunrise. I'd had a rough night and spent most of it worrying. My eyes were gritty and my head throbbed. I rolled over and tried to go back to sleep. Daylight filtered between cracks in the curtains and birdsong floated through the open window. I tossed and fidgeted until finally I gave up. I threw back the duvet and rolled out of bed. After a quick wash, I got dressed then let myself quietly out of the cabin.

On impulse I took the path behind it that ran alongside Loch Calness. A clear, bright sky signalled yet another hot day to come, but right now it was just as I liked it. After a while I stopped, slipped my feet out of my pumps and waded into the loch. The water was cold and made my feet and ankles tingle. It was so good that I shivered with delight. The view was almost drinkable. The loch's outline, following a soft rectangle, was fringed with trees of both the broad leaf and needled variety. Sunlight shone in long, straight rays onto the deep blue, almost flat, surface of the water and made it sparkle in a way that made me think of sapphires. A small bird swam in the shallows and every now and then it gave a joyful screech. I completely understood. The sheer beauty of the morning made me want to cry out too. For a short while it didn't matter who I was, or wasn't. To just be here, on this glorious day, was enough. With a happy sigh I continued to walk around the short side of the loch. When I reached the long side I left the path and cut through the trees. I kept going until I reached the double-fronted glass and wood door of the Margaret Becker building. I hadn't planned to play my flute but now I was here I wanted to.

But of course, the building was locked. Disappointment rose inside me. The desire to play my flute was too strong to let me walk away. My eyes flicked to the door as I assessed the locks, a Yale in the middle with a deadbolt beneath. They were so easy to crack it was almost a crime!

I relaxed my muscles, starting with the ones in my feet and working upwards, until in a matter of seconds I was completely tranquil. I kept my breathing slow and steady as I concentrated on the Yale lock. When I reached out with my mind it was easy to engage it. I held it firmly and forced it to open. The lock was well maintained and obediently clicked back, but I needed to hold it like that while I unlocked the deadbolt. I took a long slow breath then reached out for the second lock. There was that weird tugging sensation, of my mind splitting to work independently, and then I was able to hold the Yale open with the left side while I slid back the deadbolt with the right. I reached for the door handle, pushed it down and the door swung open. Silence greeted me. Silence and a small red light that winked down from a box near the door.

Check for intruder alarms.

It was that voice again, and the warning it rapped out almost stopped my heart. How could I have been so stupid! The building was alarmed. I should have dealt with the alarm system *before* I'd broken in. Now, I was in an impossible position. I had a matter of seconds to silence the alarm before the game was up.

ELEVEN

I didn't panic. My heartbeat accelerated but my head remained perfectly clear as I worked out what to do. A swift look around revealed a second larger box on the opposite wall. That had to be the alarm's control panel. I flipped open the cover, using my mind, and revealed a keypad. I hesitated. A part of me thought I could crack the code. But this wasn't the time to experiment; far quicker to disable the siren. My mind was ahead of me. The plastic casing over the winking red light was already turning as I mentally unscrewed it. On tiptoes I peered inside. It was a simple system and easily disabled by breaking two metal contacts. This time I used my fingers to deftly part the contacts so that it would stop the alarm from sounding. Job done! My mind was still holding the plastic casing in the air. As I let it drop into my hand, the enormity of my actions hit me. I'd broken into a building with the panache of a professional criminal.

And now, while all I really wanted was to go and play my flute, my brain was busy at work to cover my tracks. I felt like a passenger in my own body. My fingers flew over the alarm's control panel as they reset it, to prevent it from sounding when I reassembled the siren. It was awesome. And terrifying! I didn't want to think about how I'd learned these skills. I left the alarm assembled but switched off and went to collect my flute from the instrument cupboard. I took it along the corridor to practice room 4. It was my favourite room as it had a window that looked out over the woods. Sunlight poured through the glass and the room felt stuffy even at this early hour. I propped the door open with a chair, rather than waste time working out how to switch on the air con – even though it probably would have been a walk in the park after the break in! The urge to make music was so strong that my fingers trembled as I took the pieces of flute from its velvet-lined box and assembled them. I lifted the mouthpiece to my lips and the tension drained away. I felt my shoulders relax as I blew over the mouthpiece. A low note resonated around the room. It was almost as good as coming home, and it allowed me to push all thoughts of my criminal tendencies aside. I played a few, perfunctory warm-up exercises then, skipping the scales, began to perform my favourite pieces. Old ones first, followed by all the new tunes I'd learned here at Waterside, including 'The Sailor's Hornpipe'. It was fun, but subconsciously I knew I was leading up to one special piece. At last I couldn't hold out any longer. My fingers quivered as I began to play the love song that was haunting me. The first mellow notes filled the room and I let them carry me away.

It was my best performance ever. The notes lifted me so high I felt I was flying. Colours and images swirled around me until I was satiated with happiness. I didn't want the music to end. When I reached the final bars I started again, without so much as drawing breath or resting for a beat. By the end of my second rendition I was exhausted. I wanted to play on but physically I couldn't take any more. The last note carried me back down to earth and, as it faded away, I bowed my head to savour the moment. I was too fuelled with adrenalin to stay still for long. My mind lifted the flute and sent it winging through the air. I made it spin above its velvet-lined case like a dancer. I twirled with it, balancing on one foot, until eventually I was too dizzy to carry on. I stopped spinning, then stilled the flute. I used my mind to ease the pieces carefully apart, making each piece turn a graceful somersault as I put it away.

A slow clap sounded from the doorway. The final piece of the flute clattered into the box as I spun round.

'V-e-r-r-y g-o-o-d,' drawled Holly. 'Very good indeed.'

My chest was so tight that I couldn't speak. I wanted to look away but it was impossible. Holly relished every second of my discomfort. The silence stretched between us until eventually she said, 'Who are you? Or should I say, *what* exactly are you?'

'A genius!' Dan's blonde head suddenly appeared behind Holly's. He stepped around her and came into the room.

'That was amazing. I only heard the end but it was brilliant.'

'Thanks,' I whispered.

Dan didn't seem to notice the tension in the room. The look he gave me was so intense it made me shiver. Holly's blue eyes narrowed. My legs turned woolly with dread. One word from her could destroy my new happiness. I reached out to steady myself. Dan caught hold of my arm. 'Are you okay?'

'Yes, just dizzy, from playing.'

'I'm not surprised. Come and sit down,' Dan steered me towards a chair. 'Would you like a glass of water?'

'No, thanks. I'm fine, really.'

Holly cleared her throat. 'I'm so glad I came here early and heard you play. You were brilliant. It makes me wonder what other *talents* you might be hiding, Amber.' There was a definite edge to her voice.

I stared at the floor and wished I'd told Dan the truth. He was going to hate me, not just for my weirdness but for the secrets I had kept from him.

Holly shot me a knowing smile. '*Finally* I've got what I came for. Now I'd best be off. I promised to call my dad. He loves to know what I've been up to. I must remember to tell him all about you, Amber! See you at breakfast.'

'Yes.' My voice came out in a croak. 'See you later.'

Holly sent me one last, triumphant look before she left. I stood up slowly. Why had she held back and not told Dan about me? What was her plan? Not knowing felt even worse than if she had said something.

'I'd better go too,' I said.

'Must you?' Dan stepped closer. 'I've been trying to get you alone for days. Anyone would think you've been avoiding me.'

'Why would I do that?' My words sounded hollow.

'Oh, I don't know. Maybe you thought that you were cramping my style?' Dan paused. 'I could have done with your company. Holly's been driving me mad. She's worse than a second shadow.'

'Really?'

'Really.'

Dan leaned towards me. We were so close that our noses were almost touching. A tingle raced up my spine. Was he going to kiss me? He bent his head and I half closed my eyes. His lips stopped a millimetre from mine. There was a beat when neither of us breathed. A shadow crossed his face and slowly he drew back. He lifted his hand and pushed a strand of hair away from my face. His fingers brushed softly against my cheek.

My face burned with longing. I wanted to grab his hand and keep it there. But I had no right to. Not until I'd told him the truth. I opened my mouth to begin. Then a strange thought came to me. Who was I hiding from? What if my past was so terrible that the accident had given me the perfect opportunity to hide? The words died on my lips. I stared at Dan and was suddenly unable to speak.

'I'm sorry,' he whispered. 'I'm rushing things.' He made it sound like a statement, but his eyes were asking a question.

I remained silent. What could I say? Disappointment flickered across his face; he stepped back creating a distance between us. As if the past moments were of no significance, he asked casually, 'How did you get in? Did Mum lend you a key?'

I wanted to be honest with him. I really did. But the stakes were too high. 'The building was open.'

'That's not possible. I locked up last night. I remember setting the alarm.'

'Are you sure? Who else has keys? Perhaps one of the teachers came back for something and forgot to lock up again.'

Dan shook his head, disbelief written all over his face. 'Only the full-time teachers have keys. They always remember to lock up. Everyone knows to be careful. There is thousands of pounds worth of equipment in here.'

I shrugged. 'Mistakes happen. Nothing was stolen, no harm done.'

Dan was perplexed. 'No harm done this time! I'll have to mention it to Mum though. She'll want to remind everyone to be extra careful. Grand scale theft of the instruments would not be good for the business.'

Was I a thief? I was used to nice things: people driers, touch screen computers, my beautiful amber necklace. If my memory returned would I want to steal from Dan's family? Suddenly it was too difficult to be in the same room as him.

'I have to go.'

'Amber...'

I turned back.

Dan paused. He looked as if he'd been going to tell me something important but all he said was, 'I'll walk with you to Chopin.'

On the way back Dan told me that students used to keep their instruments in the cabins, until at one summer school, a boy had played his trombone all through the night. 'He was a genius, but pretty weird with it.'

'Like me?' I hadn't meant to speak aloud.

Dan touched my arm and said huskily, 'I'd never call you weird.'

Not now he wouldn't. But what if Holly spilled my secret? I had an inkling that she was building up to something. What if she decided to go public about me at breakfast, when she had a bigger audience than just Dan? I thought about skipping breakfast but I had to eat at some point. If Holly was going to expose me I might as well get it over with. I got to the dining hall ahead of her. When she finally appeared, with Erin hopping at her heels, she chose a table on the opposite side of the room to Lucy, Josh, Amy, Ellie, George and me. I chewed half-heartedly on a piece of toast. What was she playing at? It didn't make sense unless, having been made to look stupid once at the hospital, she was biding her time until she had further proof of my weirdness.

That was it. A simple explanation, but weren't simple ideas often the best ones? As I swallowed my toast I realised it wasn't just Holly that I was thinking about now. For weeks I'd struggled to make my mobile phone work. I'd searched for increasingly complicated and sophisticated ways to unlock it. But what if the solution wasn't complicated at all? Suddenly I had a theory I needed to test. I stacked my half-finished mug of coffee on the plate with the remains of my toast, and stood up.

'Not hungry?' asked Lucy, who was enthusiastically tucking into a bowl of cereal laced with fresh raspberries.

'Not at all,' I said truthfully. 'I've a couple of jobs to do before my music lesson. You don't mind if I go, do you?'

'I think we can manage, can't we, Josh?'

Josh looked up from a mug of tea and nodded. He wasn't much of a conversationalist first thing in the morning.

'See you later, then.'

'Later,' agreed Lucy, with a wave.

I ditched my dirty crockery on a trolley then raced back to Chopin. Back in my room I dragged the corner of my bed away from the wall and jammed it against the door, where I sat on it. There was no way anyone would get in without a struggle. I eased my mobile phone out of my pocket. My chest felt so tight I could hardly breathe. It was no good telling myself to calm down. There was too much at stake. If my theory worked, I was on the verge of finding out exactly who I was. I held my hand out flat so that I could see the phone clearly. I focused my mind and asked it to take hold of the phone. Nothing! I might as well have asked the sun to stop shining.

That wasn't right. I should be able to use my mind to

touch anything I wanted to. I suddenly noticed how tense I was. I took some deep breaths, holding each one in before I huffed the air out. It made me light headed but I could feel my muscles relaxing. I maintained the deep breathing until finally I was able to reach out with my mind and grip the phone.

Turn on.

It was that easy. The pale screen lit up obediently. Six empty boxes appeared, each with two words beneath them. I didn't recognise the language. Frustration bit me so hard that I nearly threw the phone across the room. That wouldn't help! I shut my eyes and when I reopened them I'd calmed down. Okay, so the blank boxes were for me to fill in a passcode. This was *my* mobile. I had to know the code! I tapped the first box with my finger. A small keypad appeared on screen. I trusted my mind to help, giving it full control of my fingers. After a few seconds my fingers started to type. They moved so fast that I only caught the first two letters of the password – the letter 'A' followed by the letter 'M'. It had to be coincidence; they were also the first letters of my new name!

The boxes disappeared from the screen. A tiny dot appeared in the centre and from it an explosion of colour rained down the screen. Next a menu flashed up, a stack of square boxes in a variety of colours. Each box had an identifying icon in the middle and a foreign word I didn't recognise underneath. Two of the boxes had a violent purple number attached to their top corner, the number ten and the number six.

I stared at the screen. What did it mean? The harder I tried to work it out the bigger the puzzle became. At last I stepped back from the problem. It was hard, but for ages I forced myself to simply sit and look at the screen. Then, unbelievably, the fog cleared. My heart lifted. I grinned like an idiot. I understood the writing underneath the icons.

The rectangular symbol, with the wavy line, had the word 'phone' written beneath it and the large purple six meant that I'd missed that many calls. The dots, arranged in a pyramid, had the word 'texts' under it. I had ten. I swallowed fearfully as my finger hovered over the screen. Here I was, merely seconds away from learning my true identity. And what then? Would that knowledge blow my world apart for a second time? The pressure in my head was like a band of iron slowly tightening. For a long time I didn't move. Curiosity won out. I had to know.

So what should I look at first, text messages or missed calls? That was easy. I needed information before I could cope with speaking to someone from my past. With trembling hands, I pressed the text messages icon.

TWELVE

I skipped my flute lesson with Mr Mason. I excused myself by saying that I had a headache. It was almost the truth. There was so much stuff in my brain that it was at bursting point. While everyone else crowded into the practice rooms I slipped away. I followed the trees hemming the east side of the loch until I found a secluded spot by the water. I sat down, with my back propped against a tree trunk, and stared across the lake while my scattered thoughts assembled into some kind of order.

The texts had told me everything. Yet nothing. My first name was Amara, my travelling companion, Nell. Somewhere out there, two people were missing us: Tor and Nardo. Their names were blank spaces. I tried hard to remember them but I couldn't. Nardo had signed his name with two kisses. His text wasn't personal so I hoped that we were just friends. It felt weird enough not remembering Amara. I didn't need her boyfriend to cope with as well. The big question though, the one I wanted answered more than anything else in the world, was this. What had I got myself into?

While the initial texts from Tor and Nardo were the

kind of stuff that friends might send, the last one, that arrived just minutes before I worked out how to access my phone, was frankly more... sinister. Maybe I was being paranoid but I didn't think so. When you looked at the evidence things didn't look great for me. I had no other messages on my mobile at all. My address book was empty. What kind of person has a totally empty address book? Even geeks have contacts. So unless the mobile had been damaged in the accident, the only explanation was that the phone was one I was using for something illicit.

I pulled it out of my pocket. I tapped the messages icon and scrolled through Tor's texts until I reached his last one.

Need to know you are on task and have not been compromised. RING ME.

I stared at the screen and my lips soundlessly repeated the words.

Need to know you are on task.

What task? How might I be compromised? Who exactly was I? Junior spy or...

I forced myself to say the word out loud: 'Criminal.'

All at once I was taken with a sudden urge to hurl the mobile phone into the water. I didn't have to be Amara. I was Amber now. I had new friends and a new life. But even as I swung my arm back, desperate to consign the phone to the very deepest part of Loch Calness, I knew it didn't work like that. I could hide from my past. But one day, probably when I least expected it, my past would find me again. It was better to confront it and deal with it now. When things were sorted out and I'd paid for any misdemeanours that I'd committed, then I could carry on being Amber.

The first step was to ring Tor. Panic clenched my stomach. What would I say? How could I even begin to explain to a stranger, by phone, what had happened to Nell and me? Maybe I should text him first? It wasn't a coward's solution, not given the circumstances. Texting was a good idea. I'd ask to meet up. When I saw a familiar face my memory might return and all this madness finally make sense. My finger hovered over the screen. What if I texted Tor and he rang me back? How awkward would that be? I suppose I didn't have to answer, but it would look suspicious if I didn't. I called up Nardo's texts and re-read them. They were less formal than Tor's. They came with kisses. Nardo sounded like a friend, whereas Tor seemed more like the boss. It would be better to make contact with Nardo first. I composed and deleted several texts before I found the right words.

Having a few difficulties. Can we meet?

Then, before I could change my mind, I quickly hit 'send'.

Nardo must have been sitting on his mobile. I nearly had a heart attack when a minute later a text pinged back.

Tomorrow. Rosie's Cafe. Balochry. 1.30 p.m. Nxx

Tomorrow! But that was good, wasn't it?

When I'd woken up in hospital, all those weeks ago, I would have given anything to know who I was. Now I wasn't so sure. I'd got used to this new me. I liked being Amber. I loved my new life. Would I like the old one as much? A thousand questions crowded into my head. I seized on ones that came with answers. I called up the internet on my phone and discovered that Balochry was a Highland town, approximately 65 kilometres from Kirkgreen. There was a bus that went from Kirkgreen to Edinburgh, and a train from there to Balochry. Now I needed an excuse to leave Waterside for a day. It wasn't long before my devious brain came up with a plan. Claudia and her parents were travelling in the area. I would tell Mia and Jeff that I'd been invited to join them.

I hated lying to the Marshalls, especially when both Mia and Jeff offered to drive me to Edinburgh where I'd said that I was meeting Claudia. They were really persuasive

150

and I had a hard time convincing them I'd rather make my own way there. Lucy thought I was mad.

'You seriously want to catch a bus when someone's offering you a lift?' she asked, as we queued in the dining hall for lunch.

'At least let me drive you to the Kirkgreen bus stop,' said Dan, who'd joined the queue behind us.

I thought about refusing. I'd been going to call a taxi, but something in the way he was looking at me made it impossible. 'That would be great, thanks.'

Dan's smile lit up his blue eyes. It was nice how pleased he seemed.

'Hi Dan,' Holly joined the queue behind him. She touched his arm and her perfect red nails skimmed across his tanned skin. 'What's for lunch?'

A muscle twitched in Dan's jaw. In a friendly voice he answered, 'Hot dogs, I think.'

'In that case I'll just grab a salad. Hi, Amber,' Holly's gaze slid over to me and speared me dead. 'That was really *something* this morning.'

My insides stilled. After breakfast, I'd convinced myself that Holly was biding her time and waiting for more evidence before she busted my secret. I must have severely overestimated her ability to keep quiet.

To overestimate the enemy is arguably more dangerous than to underestimate him or her.

As the words ran through my head I had a fleeting memory of where I'd first heard them, but it was gone before I could catch it.

A small smile played at Holly's lips. I kept my face impassive. I was determined not to give her the satisfaction of reacting when she told everyone what she'd seen. But Holly was like a sharp-clawed cat with a tiny mouse and she hadn't finished playing with me yet.

'What?' asked Lucy. 'What was really something?'

Holly's eyes never left mine. 'Amber and her flute. Ask her to show you what she can do with it sometime.'

'The bus station is over there.' Dan pulled up his car alongside the pavement and switched off the engine. 'Shall I walk you over the road?'

I looked out of the window. The bus stop wasn't what I'd expected. It was very primitive and consisted of a metal pole with a sign at the top.

'I'll be fine from here, but thanks for the lift.'

'Anytime. I'll drive you to Edinburgh if you want.'

'Thanks, but…' I chose my words with care. 'It's time I started doing things for myself.'

I reached for the door but for some reason, probably nerves, I couldn't get it open. Dan unfastened his seat belt and stretched a muscular arm across me to help me. As the door swung wide he reached out and ran his finger lightly down my cheek.

'Amber,' he stared into my eyes. 'You don't have to be alone. If you need anything, or you want a lift back from Edinburgh, call me.'

I almost melted. I had a sudden urge to grab his hand and ask him to drive me to Balochry and meet Nardo with me. Guilt gnawed at my stomach. I hated lying to Dan again, but I couldn't tell him the truth until I knew what I was hiding.

I was early for the bus and the only person waiting at the stop. On the other side of the road Dan went into the newsagent. He turned and waved as he disappeared inside. My hand strayed to my face as I remembered his touch. I ached for everything to turn out right. I wanted Nardo and Tor to be friends, and for the whole spy or criminal thing to be either a stupid game, or the crackpot result of a mind damaged by a traumatic accident. I wasn't aware that a dark saloon had pulled up alongside me until the passenger's window slid down. A bald-headed, middle-aged man called out, 'Excuse me lass. The bus has been delayed. Would you like a lift somewhere?'

I checked my watch. I'd planned to get to the train station early so I still had plenty of time. On the other hand,

I could grab Dan when he came out of the newsagents and ask him to drive me to Edinburgh. With a polite smile I answered, 'No, thanks.'

I was watching out for Dan and was unprepared for the speed with which the man jumped out of the car. He wrapped me in a steely grip and bundled me onto the back seat. It took a few seconds to realise I was being kidnapped. I lashed out with my feet but it was too late. They crunched against the car door as it slammed shut.

'Help!' I screamed.

I banged on the window with one hand while I fumbled for the door handle with the other.

'Sit down. Shut up!' As the car sped away Baldy turned to face me. I would have happily argued with him but not with the small black handgun he was pointing at me.

My heart raced and blood sang in my ears. I felt light-headed and detached. It was almost as if the drama was happening to someone else. After a few seconds something clicked inside me. The turmoil stilled and my head cleared. I quickly stared out of the window to memorise the route we were travelling. We left Kirkgreen on the opposite side of the town to the one I was familiar with. At the roundabout we took the third exit off the roundabout and entered a dual carriageway. The road was signed Livingstone and Bathgate. Baldy turned in his seat.

His neck and head flushed a violent shade of red. 'Get down,' he bellowed and waved the gun in my face.

I bowed my head but not quickly enough. Baldy hit me between the shoulder blades with the gun's handle. 'Right down! On the floor and stay there. She was reading the road signs,' he explained to the driver.

My back hurt like hell. Resentment curdled in my gut. I crouched on the floor, with my knees drawn up, and hoped that I wasn't going to be sick. The car sped on. It lurched round corners and crashed over bumps in the road. I knew that Baldy still had his gun trained on me. I hoped he had a steady finger. Something, from the hidden depths of my memory, informed me that the gun didn't have a safety catch. After a long, agonising ride the car slowed and then turned left. The road surface changed from smooth to bumpy. I gritted my teeth. We were travelling along some kind of lane or driveway. The car slowed, turned and, thankfully, jolted to a stop.

'We're here,' said Baldy, as the engine died. 'You can get up now.'

I stared apprehensively out of the window. I'm not sure what I was expecting, but it wasn't this. We were parked on the gravelled drive of a neat stone house with a grey slate roof. Baldy trained the gun at my head. 'Empty your pockets.'

Much as I wanted to refuse to co-operate I wasn't that stupid. I meekly handed over my purse.

'And the rest.'

It had been worth a try! With a greater reluctance I gave up my mobile phone. Money was easy to replace but the phone was my only means of communication with the people from my past. I wondered if Baldy and his friend knew who I was. It wasn't a comfortable thought.

'Get out of the car. Slowly. No sudden moves.'

I didn't like the way Baldy's hand shook, so I did as he'd asked, with an emphasis on slow. It was no surprise that the house was set in the middle of a large garden, bordered with hedges and trees. There weren't any houses near by, so no neighbours to hear my cries for help. The driver unlocked the front door, wiggling the key when it got stuck. He was tall, with fair hair, pale blue eyes and fleshy bags of skin underneath. There was something familiar about him. I tried to recall if he came from my old life or my new one, as he forced the door open with his shoulder.

'In you go.' Baldy pushed me over the threshold. The house was clean, but the air smelled stale and there was a faint whiff of damp. It was obvious that no one had lived here for a while. On the table, in the hallway, rested a small box of groceries. A label on the side bore the logo of a canal boat and the words, Falkirk Holiday Homes. Baldy shoved me past the table and upstairs. At the top of the staircase he directed me to a room at the front of the house.

I was so scared I almost couldn't breathe, but I wasn't going into the room without some show of resistance. I stood in the doorway, feet astride. 'Who are you? What do you want?'

'All in good time,' Baldy pushed me and I almost fell over. I spun round on instinct, ready to disarm him but my reactions were a fraction too slow. The door slammed shut in my face. The key turned in the lock. Footsteps sounded down the creaky stairs. There was a muffled conversation in the hallway and then the front door banged shut. I crossed over to the window and watched Baldy and the driver climb into the car. I just had time to note the number plate, and commit it to my photographic memory, before the car drove away. I leaned on the windowsill and watched until it had gone. At first I was too stunned to move. Who had done this to me? And more importantly why? I was outraged, but at the same time I couldn't help being impressed at the efficiency and smooth execution of the kidnapping. Someone obviously knew about my travel plans. Who though? The only people that knew about my trip by bus to Edinburgh were my friends at Waterside. And Nardo.

The thought was as welcome as a rat in a sweet shop. When I'd texted Nardo to confirm our rendezvous he'd asked where I was coming from. Without thinking I'd given him the details of my bus and train trip. But why would Nardo arrange to have me kidnapped at gunpoint? It didn't make sense. Not to me, but what about Amara? Did she know what was going on? Fear squeezed my insides until I felt like I was suffocating. I needed air. I tried to open the window, but it was locked. I would have cheerfully broken it but, apart from a neatly made bed and an empty wardrobe, there was nothing in the room to break it with. I was on the verge of hyperventilating.

In times of crisis what's the golden rule?

The dark-haired woman appeared in my mind.

'Stay calm,' I choked back.

Her eyes flicked to mine and she smiled her approval. When her image died I was left with renewed courage. I could and would escape.

THIRTEEN

I perched on the end of the bed while I considered what to do next. Things weren't looking great. I was a prisoner. I had no idea where I was, or who was holding me. Worse still, I didn't know what my kidnappers wanted with me. For a while I explored my earlier theory that Nardo had kidnapped me, but the more I thought about it the more unlikely it seemed. What would be the point? He could have been trying to scare me but that seemed unlikely. His texts had been friendly, and he sounded relieved to hear from me. I'd agreed to meet him, so why would he go to the bother of stealing me away? No, Nardo wasn't responsible for my current predicament. But he did have answers about my previous life. It was essential that I kept our rendezvous.

Breaking in to places was my speciality. I'd proved that yesterday when I'd broken into the Margaret Becker building. By that reckoning, if I could break in to a building then I must be capable of breaking out again. I jumped off the bed and was at the door in a few strides. I was so fired up that I was practically burning. I forced myself to stay calm while I reached out with my mind and asked it to grasp the lock. It was a standard tubular latch, nickel plated, and freshly oiled. It slid back with ease. The bedroom, like the rest of the house, had a musty, unlived feel about it. The front door had stuck in the frame. I should have thought to question why the lock was so well maintained, but I didn't. Flushed with my success, I stood on the landing and did a mental dance of victory. Then I hopped down the stairs, taking them two at a time. In the hall I forced open the front door and ran outside into the sunshine.

Baldy and the driver were waiting for me. The driver raised his eyebrows and Baldy nodded. His grin was so wide that it almost severed his face. My escape had been a set-up! I could have stamped my feet in frustration. I needed every ounce of self-control I possessed, to stand tall and face my kidnappers with dignity.

'We'd heard that you were *special*.' The driver could hardly contain his excitement. 'Holly's a good girl. I knew she wasn't exaggerating.'

Holly had betrayed me. She hated me because I was different and my weirdness frightened her. I'd got her into trouble at the hospital. But to get me kidnapped was pretty extreme. Most girls Holly's age would have stuck to bullying me.

'I can see you're confused. Let's go back to your room

for a wee chat.'

I didn't move. Should I make a run for it? There was no sign of the gun and I was fit, from all the exercise I'd been doing. I could easily outrun Baldy and his paunchy friend. Baldy watched me closely. Suddenly he lunged and grabbed my arm. He twisted it behind my back. I bit my lip rather than give him the satisfaction of crying out in pain.

'Upstairs,' he hissed.

His breath reeked of onions and stale tobacco. I did as I was told, mutinously dragging my feet as I walked up the stairs. My heart sank as I entered the bedroom again. I'd only just escaped from here. Why hadn't I been more cautious? It was a stupid mistake to underestimate my enemies. Baldy forced me to sit on the bed. He and the driver towered over me. It was an old interrogation tactic. Make the captive feel small. I mentally made myself bigger and refused to be cowed.

'Introductions first,' the driver held out his nicotine-stained hand. 'I'm Robert Jenkins.'

Jenkins. Where had I heard that name before? Then I got it. 'You're Holly's father.' There was a strong family resemblance.

'Smart lass! This is my brother, Johnny Jenkins.' Johnny held out his hand but I kept mine firmly in my lap. He sniggered. Robert shrugged as if shaking hands with them made no difference either way.

'And you are?'

'Amber.' He must already know that.

'Amber who?'

'I don't know.'

'Oh, come on. Let's drop the pretence. What's your full name, lass?'

'I don't know my full name. So, for now, it's Amber, and I'm not your lass,' I snapped back.

Robert and Johnny exchanged a look of surprise.

'You really don't know who you are? How *very* interesting!' Robert walked to the window. He turned with a deliberate slowness, and then leaned against the sill so that he was looking straight at me. Sunlight illuminated his profile, silvering the grey flecks in his hair. His face was partially shadowed and it softened his wrinkles and made him look younger. He must have been handsome once, if Holly was anything to go by.

'I don't understand why no one has missed you. You're very special. Or have you learned to keep your *uniqueness* a secret, to fit in? It must be awful to be the freak.'

He sounded as if he was talking to himself. Just as well because I had no intention of answering any questions. The silence played out until at last he pushed himself upright and took a step closer. 'Let me tell you something about my position. I'm an accountant. Financially I'm comfortable. I've made extra money by taking a creative approach with those of my clients who aren't shy about breaking rules. Over the years, we've done some good deals. Very good! It's been easy money. I've brought you here because I want to offer you a slice of something similar. Call it the chance of a lifetime. With your talents and our business acumen,' a nod at Johnny showed the 'our' included him too, 'we'd make a formidable team. There'd be no stopping us. I'm not talking creative accounting now. I'm thinking much bigger, a good, old-fashioned heist with an extrasensory twist. Just think, your telekinetic skills combined with our business expertise – we could have riches beyond our dreams.'

'Except that I already have riches beyond *your* dreams.' The words came from nowhere. They were as much of a surprise to me as they were to Robert and Johnny. I shut my mouth. I didn't have a clue what I was talking about and I was filled with unease. Something told me I'd just let slip not just any old secret, but one of major importance.

'Is that so?' Excitement and triumph blazed from Robert's eyes. He spoke slowly, emphasising his words. 'Then, when you do finally remember your name, you'll also remember who will want to share those riches with us to ensure your safe return.'

The silence that followed was suffocating.

'Sleep on it,' he added.

He left the room abruptly. Johnny followed and their heavy footsteps receded down the stairs. The front door grunted open and then shut and I heard footsteps on the drive as they left together. There was no point locking me in, but to leave me here unguarded – was it another trap?

I went to the window and watched Robert and Johnny stride round the side of the house. They'd come on foot, which explained why I hadn't heard the car return. It also meant they hadn't come far. I shot out of the room and ran into the one opposite. It was another bedroom and the window looked out onto a long, overgrown garden. Tucked away in the bottom corner was a blue sun house. Robert and Johnny crossed the lawn and, walking quickly, they entered the building. I watched for a little while longer, but there was nothing more to see. Deep in thought I returned to the original bedroom and began to search it. I had no idea what I was looking for, but instinct told me that I'd missed something important.

The cream-coloured room was unremarkable. It was furnished with a single bed, a pine wardrobe, a dressing table and a chair. The lamp base on the dressing table was also made of pine and the shade was made of a green synthetic fabric. There was another light fixed to the ceiling, a wavy, brushed pewter bar with three equally spaced LED spotlights fixed to it. My heart did a double beat. It wasn't an ordinary light fitting. I flopped down on the bed and studied it furtively, through my eyelashes. It was just as I thought. The middle spotlight was split in two: one side was a light and the other the sort of camera that records moving images. So that was why Robert and Johnny had left me unguarded. They were sneakily viewing my every move from their little hut in the garden. I was almost as annoyed about the invasion of my privacy as I was about the kidnap. It was tempting to disable the camera, in the same way that I'd silenced the alarm in the Margaret Becker building, but something was telling me not to act in haste. I lay on the bed while I worked out an escape plan. At last I had it. It was incredibly simple, as the best plans are.

Robert and Johnny might think I was still resting but my feet were carefully easing off my shoes and socks. Once I was barefooted I didn't move again for ages.

The next phase was to create a diversion. I sat up and yawned as I swung my legs over the side of the bed. I walked to the window where I made a show of feeling round the wooden frame and tapping at the glass. It took great control not to glance at the camera as I continued my examination. Meanwhile, my mind was busy moving my socks along the floor. When they reached the door my mind lifted them up until they were touching the ceiling. I needed to see the light fitting for the next part of my plan. I continued to tap at the window but turned my head until I could see the socks from the corner of my eye. I hoped Robert and Johnny were still enjoying my antics. While they were watching me, my mind was busy guiding an incoming pair of stripy socks towards the hidden camera. Any second now and they'd be landing.

The instant my mind released the socks, effectively blacking out the camera, I grabbed my shoes and ran. I sped down the stairs, jumping the last few, and landed halfway up the hall. As I burst out of the front door I was met with a wall of warm air, heavy with the scent of pollen.

It took half a second to acclimatise to the heat and another half to assess the best route of escape. The driveway was clearly the quickest way, but it was very exposed. A dense jungle of bushes and trees lay to the side of the house. It offered brilliant cover but would be harder to navigate and I wasn't sure where it would take me. My brain processed the options. To use the drive would be suicide. I might as well hand myself straight over to Robert and Johnny now. Decision made, I ran towards the trees. The stony ground bit into my bare feet. After a few painful steps I stopped to pull on my shoes. Then I was off again, plunging deeper into the vegetation. The further I went the more confident I became that I'd escaped. The relief was like water bursting through a dam. But over-confidence is as good as a tripwire. As I ran from one tree to another, hands grabbed me from behind.

Instinct, and the personal survival training I didn't remember taking, kicked in. I leaned back into the unknown person's arms, lifted my right foot and stamped it down on the top of my attacker's foot. He grunted in pain. I stuck out my behind and used my body weight to flip him over my head. There was a satisfying thud as he hit the ground. As I went to jump over his prostrate body a small voice called out, 'Amber.'

'Dan! Bloody hell. What are you doing here? Are you hurt?'

'Winded,' he gasped. 'I saw you get snatched. I followed you in the car.'

Dan gratefully took the hand I offered to help him up. Back on his feet, his grip tightened and he pulled me towards him. The world, along with my heartbeat, stopped. My face burned and I half-closed my eyes, my lips moving soundlessly as they came towards Dan's.

'Run!' Dan's mouth was so close to my ear that his cry

nearly burst my eardrum. As the bushes rustled and began to part I realised I was an idiot. Dan hadn't been going to kiss me at all.

'She's over here!' yelled Johnny. His clothes were covered with twigs and leaves, and his breath came in short gasps.

Embarrassment burned my cheeks. Dan still had hold of my hand and he pulled me so hard that my arm nearly came out of its socket. I stood my ground and refused to run with him. Johnny had something of mine. I wasn't going until I'd got it back.

'Amber, run.'

'Hold on.' My eyes flicked over Johnny's clothes as they scanned for pockets. He had three, one on his shirt and two in his jeans. My freaky habits didn't include seeing *through* things. I could only hope that the bulging pocket on Johnny's right thigh was the one that contained my phone and purse. I created a picture of them both in my head as I reached out with my mind. Dan was still pulling at my arm.

Lift up.

There was a soft tugging sensation as my mind split in two; then the funny grappling feeling as it sought to grip the unseen objects. It was one of the hardest lifts I'd tried. My head spun, but I forced myself to remain focused. At last Johnny's pocket began to ripple. Excitement filled me but I kept my cool and concentrated on extricating my purse and phone.

Faster.

At first Johnny's attention was all on me and he didn't notice what was happening. Dan tightened his grip on my hand, but he stopped pulling me. His eyes widened as a purse and a phone winged their way towards us. With my free hand I reached out and plucked them from the air. As I tucked them safely in my own pocket I saw the colour had drained from Dan's face. He opened and closed his mouth, but the words stayed trapped inside. I yanked at his hand.

'Run.'

I set off at speed. Johnny charged after me. He lunged and grabbed at my hair. I winced in pain as he ripped a handful from my head. Brambles scratched my legs and long-fingered branches clawed at my clothes. I battled on, towing Dan with me through the undergrowth.

'This way.' Dan suddenly pulled me sideways.

We crashed through some bushes and came out on the drive. We ran across it, dodging the potholes. There was a flash of blue through the trees.

'That's my car, over there,' said Dan.

He'd parked in a small clearing. 'Get in.' Dan pulled

his keys from his pocket. One click of a button disabled the central locking. He shoved me in through the driver's door. As I scrambled over the gear stick he clambered in after me. I was out of breath and gasping like a fish on a riverbank. I collapsed into the passenger's seat. Dan shut the door, locked it and started the engine.

'Seat belt,' he barked, as he whacked the car into reverse.

My hands fumbled with the belt; then something banged on the window. I jumped as Johnny's face appeared against the glass. Eyes wild, nostrils dilated, he hammered and kicked at the side of the car. Dan skidded out of the clearing and onto the drive. He swerved to avoid the dark saloon that came at us head on. Robert was at the wheel. He slowed and Johnny leapt inside. There was a smell of burning rubber as Robert performed a handbrake turn. Dust rose in clouds as the car screamed after us.

FOURTEEN

The driveway wasn't designed for two cars but somehow Robert managed to pull his alongside us. He swerved violently to force us off the road and into the bushes. Dan's jaw tightened. He hung on to the steering wheel and pressed his foot down hard on the accelerator. He hunched forward, as if that would make us go faster. There was a metallic shriek as the cars touched. Dan's foot was flat on the floor, the two cars neck and neck, when Johnny drew his gun.

Dan's knuckles whitened. 'Amber, down,' he growled.

I looked across at Johnny. He grinned back at me in an evil, cat's-got-the-baby-birdie kind of way, but I was over my initial shock of seeing a real weapon and more ready to take chances. My mind flew to the handgun and gripped hold of it. Slowly, I forced the gun round until it was pointing at Johnny's heart. His surprise was priceless. The colour leached from his face and his smile drained away. He recovered himself quickly though and fought against me, using both hands to swivel the gun back my way. He was very strong. It took everything I had to push the barrel back again.

Dan's head was like a metronome. 'A-a-are you doing that?' he stuttered.

'Yeah.'

I couldn't keep it up for much longer, but one glance at Johnny told me he couldn't either. His eyes were bulging and a muscle in his neck twitched repeatedly. One of us was about to break and it wasn't going to be me. I kept my mind firmly on the gun as I reached inside myself, deeper than I'd ever dared to go before. The energy flowed from my mind, hot as molten lava. It honed in on the gun and allowed me to prise it free from Johnny's rigid grip. He snatched for the gun as it floated away, but my reactions were faster. I spun it higher, guided it through the open car window – then let it go.

There was a tremendous bang. I was thrown forward and back again. The seat belt cut across my chest and I felt a new bruise spread across the old one. A second bang followed and the impact was even worse.

'They're ramming us,' said Dan, grimly.

Robert kept decelerating and then quickly accelerating so that his car bashed into the back of Dan's. I turned round and clutched hold of the back of the seat as he hit us again. My neck snapped and I squeaked with the pain. I undid the seat belt and hung out of the passenger's window. Where was the gun? My eyes searched the drive until I found it.

Dan was driving fast and the gun would soon be out of my mental reach. Once again, I called on my aching mind to seize hold of it. To my surprise, my mind projected back an image of bruised and swollen tissue. My head hurt so badly that I could hardly bear it. But I had to get hold of that gun. I ignored the pictures and insisted that my mind grasped the gun. The pain was unbearable. I blinked back tears. I would not let go. I wouldn't! With gritted teeth, I lifted the gun higher and aimed it at Robert's car.

Dan threw me a nervous look. 'Amber,' he breathed, so softly I almost didn't hear him. His knuckles were long past white and the veins in his arms taut like cheese wire.

'Trust me.' I took aim. As I went to pull the trigger we were rammed again. I lost my grip and the gun cart-wheeled towards the bushes. My mind reached out, frantic to get it back. I'd never caught an object moving at speed and I wasn't prepared for the crashing sensation in my head. I caught the gun just seconds before it disappeared under the bush. It was a miracle I was able to hang on but I somehow did. I couldn't see properly to fire. I clasped the gun firmly in a mind grip then wound down the window and leaned out. The blast of air took my breath away. My hair whipped across my face half blinding, half suffocating me. I shoved it back, tucking as much of it as I could down the neck of my T-shirt. There was another crash as Robert rammed us again. This time I'd anticipated the blow. I gripped hold of the door and let my hands take some of the impact. I still couldn't see clearly enough to shoot. I started to ease my upper body out of the window and had to fight against the rush of air that met me. Dan shouted something, but the wind was buzzing in my ears and I couldn't make it out. Trees passed, too close for comfort. A branch came towards me, at garrotting height, and I only just ducked in time.

'Amber, get back in the car. Now!' blasted Dan.

No way. Not when I could see my target. I held the gun steady then used a different part of my mind to squeeze the trigger. There was an almighty bang. Robert's car slewed violently. I saw his hands tighten on the wheel as he fought to correct the steering. I aimed again and claimed his three remaining tyres. Sparks flew like Catherine wheels as Robert continued to drive on the wheel rims. A short while later the car slowed then shuddered to a stop. I was shaking badly and wanted to be rid of the gun for good. I hurled it at the uppermost branches of a very tall tree and gave it a hard shove with my mind to help it along. It stuck in the top branch and I smiled in relief. I was confident that Robert and Johnny wouldn't be able to climb that high to get it back. Relieved that for now the fight was over, I pulled myself back into the car. My muscles ached and I had a colossal headache. We were almost at the end of the drive, not that Dan showed any sign of slowing down. He pulled straight out onto the main road and almost took out the rear end of a passing car, as he slotted behind it. My head hurt too badly to care. I stared vacantly ahead and let my ragged mind go blank.

We drove for several kilometres until, entering a forest of tall pine trees, Dan pulled off the road and into a car park. He drove past the cars lined up by the entrance and parked in the corner. As he cut the engine a loud silence filled the void. Apart from cars, the car park was empty. Even the birds in the trees had flown away when Dan screeched into the parking space. The silence grew and its loudness hurt my ears.

'Well?' he said finally. He didn't look at me but stared out of the window and into the thick, green forest. 'Want to explain what's going on?'

His voice, and the dull look in his eyes, made my chest tighten. He was hurt and it was my fault. My throat constricted, so that when I spoke my voice wasn't the one I'd grown accustomed to.

'I'm sorry. I wanted to tell you about me but...'

But what? I hadn't trusted him with my secrets even though he'd shared his with me? I breathed deeply then started again. 'I wanted to tell you about me for ages, but it's complicated…'

Once I got going it was much easier than I'd imagined. I told Dan everything. I confessed to all the fears and doubts that had gnawed away at me since I discovered how different I was from anyone else. Dan listened in silence. Occasionally he'd nod, or a knowing look would flash across his face. I felt like I was handing him chunks of an enormous puzzle that he'd been working on for ages.

'So that's it,' I finished. 'I have to get to Balochry and see Nardo. Then I'll know who Amara is.'

'I'll take you,' said Dan. Just like that. No questions, no recriminations. I'd lied, almost smashed up his car and nearly got him killed. Yet he still wanted to help me.

'What about my telekinetic powers, don't they freak you out?'

'Yes, at first. When I saw your purse and mobile fly through the air, it was beyond creepy. I didn't know what to think. It was like you'd turned into a mad spirit, or something. I nearly turned tail and ran. Then I reasoned that you'd had plenty of time to do me harm if you wanted to. And the bald guy, Johnny, deserved what he was getting. Kidnap and theft! The gun thing was the worst part, though. I thought you were going to kill him when you took control of it. I was with my grandad when he died. It was a peaceful death and that was bad enough.'

Dan gave a shaky laugh. 'Aiding and abetting homicide, how would that look on my UCAS form?' He looked into my eyes. 'I'm glad you didn't kill anyone. And now I'm over the shock, I like the telekinesis. It's cool.'

'I'd never kill anyone.' It came from the bottom of my heart.

Dan squeezed my hand. 'I believe you, given your unnatural affection for Scottish enemy number one, the mosquito.'

We shared a smile.

'What if I drag you into something illegal? I don't want to ruin your chances of getting into university.'

'Amber,' said Dan, looking straight at me, 'you're too nice to be involved in anything illegal.'

'Amber might be, but what about Amara?'

'Then don't be Amara. Stick with your new life.'

If only it was that easy. 'Being Amber hasn't stopped me from being different.'

'Have you ever thought that you're different for a reason? Maybe you don't come from here?' Dan trailed off.

I nodded because subconsciously I had already worked that out. Dan spoke with a soft, Scottish burr. My accent was more lyrical. My mobile phone wasn't in English either. Come to think of it neither were Tor and Nardo's texts. How stupid of me! I'd been too worked up to rationalise that this was a massive clue to my real identity. 'I'm a foreigner, aren't I? Do you think that I might come from Europe or something?'

Dan reached out and held both of my hands in his. 'Or something,' he whispered hoarsely.

We were so close that his breath tickled my cheeks. I wondered how it would feel if he wrapped his arms around me. I wanted it so badly, it made my head spin. Dan watched me and waited for a cue to come closer. Heat crept up my cheeks. My lips tingled. I started to lean forward, but the movement set alarm bells clamouring in my head. This was all wrong. There were too many questions needing an answer before we took our relationship to the next stage. With great reluctance I pulled my hands free and reached for my mobile phone. I had to swallow hard before I could speak. 'What language is this? Do you recognise it?'

A flash of disappointment, or was it irritation, flickered in Dan's eyes. He blinked and then stared at the screen. 'Italian perhaps, or another European country. Do you understand it?'

I nodded.

'You don't have a strong accent. When I first heard you speak I thought you might originally have come from Eastern Europe, but that you'd lived in the UK for a long time.'

'What if I'm a spy? Are you sure you want to take me to Balochry? I might get you into all sorts of trouble.'

Dan laughed. 'And you haven't already! Why do you think you're a spy? That's mad. Right now, I'm here to help out a friend. Where's the harm in that?'

Dan knew the risks he was taking, but he still wanted to help me. The knowledge made my heart race much faster than was natural. 'You're totally sure about this?'

'Absolutely. No more lies, though. From now on you have to tell the truth. Promise?'

'I promise.'

'Thanks.'

Our eyes met but neither of us spoke. Trust didn't need words.

'Something tells me that this Robert and Johnny aren't going to give up on you that easily. We'd better get going before they come after us. I bet they've got another car between them and more guns.' Dan unfastened his seat belt. 'I'll just check my car before we leave.' He opened the door and climbed out. I followed and we spent several precious minutes looking over the bodywork.

Fortunately, the damage wasn't as bad as I'd feared. The bumper was dented, and there were scratches to the paintwork, but Dan didn't see any of it as a problem. 'My friend's dad repairs cars. He'll fix it for me.'

'I'll text Nardo and warn him I'm going to be late,' I said.

Dan checked his watch. 'Tell him you'll be there for 2 p.m.'

As we pulled onto the main road Nardo texted back to say he'd meet me at 4 p.m. and it would be better if I slept over. I wasn't keen on that idea, neither was Dan, but without knowing who Nardo was, I couldn't think of a good enough reason to refuse him.

'I'll tell Mum that Claudia's parents invited you to stay the night at their hotel. If the reunion doesn't go well, call me and I'll come and pick you up,' Dan said.

There was plenty of time to get to Balochry now but, for my safety, Dan wanted to get me somewhere populated, and quickly. He drove fast, his little car eating up the distance. It should have been fun, having Dan all to myself, but I was too nervous to enjoy it. I was sure that the green saloon, quite a distance behind, was tailing us. I sat with my head swivelled so that I could watch it out of the rear window. It was ages before the car went a different way and I was able to relax. After a bit I saw a smoky blue line etched on the horizon. As we drove towards it, the line became more distinctive until I could see that it was a range of mountains.

'The Highlands,' said Dan, nodding at them.

We entered a forest and its dark green canopy blotted out the view. Once we were out the other side, the road began to loop. Each twist brought another surprise in the scenery. Once, there was a stream: it was crystal clear and the water gurgled with laughter as it raced along beside the car. Another time, as the road curved, we came upon a huge loch, cupped in the hollow of a hill. The blue water shimmered like a jewel in a gigantic hand. It was so beautiful that Dan, who'd been singing along to the radio, stopped mid-song to savour the view. Much further along we drove across a wooden bridge that was covered with an archway of trees. Beams of sunlight shone down on the timber slats. They dappled the road with shadow and light and for a fleeting moment, I was somewhere else – somewhere that I couldn't quite remember. Then we were over the bridge, back in full sunlight, and the feeling slipped away to skulk, like the shadows on the bridge, in the corners of my mind.

The road climbed and, a short while later, we arrived at the outskirts of a small Highland town.

'We're here,' said Dan. He shifted into a lower gear as we swung round a bend.

The pavements were packed with holidaymakers, their

faces bright with smiles as they ambled along searching for bargains in the tiny shops. A woman with sunglasses perched on top of her head seated her family at a table on the pavement outside a coffee shop. Everywhere I looked there were people, taking time out of their normal lives, eating *gelati*, having fun. I ached to be one of them. If only I could be here with Dan for a carefree day out. For weeks my sole aim had been to find out who I was. Now, when I was about to get an answer, I didn't want to know.

FIFTEEN

Rosie's Café was on the corner of Balochry's main road and not far from the car park where we left Dan's car.

'It looks good,' said Dan. He pushed open the glass door and stepped inside. 'I'll buy you lunch.'

I stood on the pavement, too scared to follow. What if Nardo came early and caught us together? Until I knew exactly what was going on, I didn't want Dan involved. Naturally he misinterpreted my reluctance.

'Hey, it's only lunch. If it makes you feel better you can pay next time.'

There was going to be a next time. Even that thought wasn't enough to elicit more than a half-hearted smile from me. Dan made for a window seat but I managed to beat him to a table at the back, tucked away by the kitchen. 'Don't you want to look out?' he asked as he sat down opposite me.

'No, because I mightn't recognise who's looking in,' I quipped. I failed miserably in my attempt to make it sound as if I was joking.

'You worry too much. It's going to be fine.'

I wanted to believe him but couldn't shake off the

feeling that I was condemned.

The waitress came over with menus. Dan ordered a cheeseburger with fries and a side salad, while I chose a grilled chicken sandwich. We both asked for cold drinks and they came out first – each with two straws, a slice of lemon and ice cubes bobbing at the surface. Dan drank half of his drink straight away and ate heartily when the food arrived. I stirred my drink with the straws and picked at my sandwich. I couldn't stop my eyes from ping-ponging between my wristwatch and the door. At last Dan laid down his knife and fork. His eyes were on me as he cleared his throat. 'I don't have to go home. I could stay.'

'No!' I hadn't meant for my refusal to sound so vehement. 'Er... no thanks. I'll be fine. Really! I'm bound to be nervous. I don't even know who I'm meeting.'

'I understand. But there's no need to worry. I won't go until this Nardo guy shows up. Not after what happened at the Kirkgreen bus stop.'

I badly wanted to accept his offer to stay but, tempting as it was, I couldn't. My chest tightened. 'You can't,' I whispered. 'But I promise I'll be careful. No one will snatch me from here. It's too crowded.'

Dan looked as if he was about to protest, but he must have sensed my determination to meet Nardo alone. With a shrug he said, 'Fine. But promise me you'll be careful.'

'I just did. I'll be *very* careful.'

'And you'll call if you need me?'

'Yes.' I'd memorised Dan's number ages ago.

I was beginning to regret not picking a seat by the window. It was dark and stuffy here, and the smells from the kitchen were making me feel sick. I checked my watch again. Twenty minutes to go. I pushed my half-eaten food away. 'I think I'll wait outside.'

'Is that a good idea?'

'He didn't tell me to wait inside.'

Dan called for the bill and after he'd paid he took my arm and guided me to the door. The gesture was strangely intimate. I liked it a lot but as we stepped outside I lifted both hands, ostensibly to push back my hair, but in reality to shake him off without hurting his feelings.

'This is it then.' My stomach felt hollow as I smiled bravely up at him.

'Amber,' Dan spoke softly, sending tingles down my spine. His incredible blue eyes held mine as he stepped closer. An intense feeling of warmth filled me. I wanted to hold him so badly that at first I wasn't aware that I'd wrapped my arms around his waist. His body felt warm and solid. I nestled my head against his chest and wished the moment would never end. Dan stroked my hair as he pulled me even closer. I raised my head and the tips of our noses met. It sent a thousand tiny electric shocks pulsing through me. Time stood still. Dan brushed his lips ever so softly against mine. I held my breath, wanting his kisses, but as our mouths pressed together that hateful voice was suddenly back.

Never trust anyone.

I gasped and shoved Dan away with both hands. He reeled backwards and bumped into a lady with a dog. By the time he'd finished apologising to her I'd pulled myself together. The hurt in his eyes stung me like acid, but I knew I'd been right to push him away. 'I'm sorry, I didn't mean…'

Dan silenced me with a hand, as if being shoved halfway across the pavement was no big deal. He wouldn't meet my eye, though. My throat constricted and it left me utterly powerless to speak. I shouldn't have put my arms around him. That was Amber's fault. Only now I wasn't Amber. I was Amara again, whoever she was.

'See you around.' Dan smiled tightly. He sidestepped neatly into the stream of people walking along the pavement and vanished.

See you around. What did that mean? As I stared after him I was aware of a tall boy with a head of thick, curly, chestnut-brown hair approaching. His lean body was as

186

fluid as a leopard's. His brown eyes were thunderous and his face contorted into a scowl as he planted himself in front of me. 'You made it then. Where's Nell? Is she inside?'

'Nell...' I hesitated, choosing my words with care. 'Nell's not coming.'

'Oh?' He was unimpressed. 'Come on then. Follow me.'

Nardo had a rich, gravelly voice but the tone and the cold glint in his eyes made my toes curl. He was clearly displeased and I had no idea why.

'Nardo,' I said hesitantly, but he hadn't waited for an answer. I had to run to catch him before the crowd swallowed him too.

Nardo strode along, dodging tourists like a professional, until the shops thinned and, eventually, so did the people. As we approached the outskirts of town there was sufficient room on the pavement to walk alongside him. 'Where are we going?'

'Back to ours.'

That wasn't helpful. I didn't dare ask where 'ours' was because I probably should have known. Several paces later I began to panic. We'd passed the last building and the only piece of civilisation left was a car park full of cars and motor homes. Was Nardo taking me somewhere by car?

After this morning's episode I really couldn't face another journey into the unknown. I stopped suddenly and caught hold of his sleeve. 'Is Tor at yours?' I blurted out.

Nardo looked at me strangely and nodded.

'Can we talk? Now, while we're still on our own.'

'We have no secrets. You know that, Amara.'

The formal way he spoke reminded me of the lady in my flashbacks. It wasn't an auspicious start. My stomach clenched and I forced myself to breathe slowly before the panic took hold completely.

'Yes, but this is different. I really need to talk to you first, to explain.'

Nardo whipped round to face me and for a second I'm sure I saw fear in his eyes. 'What have you done?' he whispered. 'In the name of our mother, please tell me you haven't broken the Confidentiality Decree.'

Suddenly I was fearful too. What in hell's name was the Confidentiality Decree? What if I had broken it? Then I remembered how, according to one of my flashbacks, I was responsible for the safety of the world.

What if I'd failed my responsibilities?

Nardo was looking at me in disgust. He drew himself up and in a clipped voice said, 'Once we are away from the town and all these people, we will stop somewhere private. Then you can explain.'

To get away from the town, and its people, we had to walk until we'd left even the tourist trails behind. As the ground underfoot became more rugged I wished Nardo had thought to tell me to wear proper hiking boots, like his sturdy brown ones, instead of my flimsy trainers. Or should I have known that? My inappropriate footwear made me stumble over the loose stones. It didn't help that I couldn't concentrate. All I could see was the expression on Dan's face when I'd pushed him away. I followed numbly in Nardo's footsteps until, after walking for thirty minutes, he stopped at a fast-moving stream that passed under a rock face. The stream tumbled down the mountain and its frothy spumes sprayed us with a fine mist of water. Trails of vegetation hung from the rocks like green curtains of hair. Nardo stepped off the bank and waded upstream for a few paces, until he reached a slab of rock that jutted halfway across the water. He pushed aside a swath of green fronds, ducked his head then disappeared.

With great reluctance I rolled my jeans up to my knees then, gritting my teeth for courage, I followed in his steps. The water dragged and splashed at my legs until even my rolled up jeans were soaked. I dipped down under the rock and found myself in a small hollow. It was dimly lit and apart from the occasional drip of water trickling off the walls it was very quiet. You couldn't even hear the stream as it rattled by.

Nardo was perched on a stone and I sat on a smaller one by his side.

'Well,' he said, his voice tight. 'You didn't waste time. Who's the boy?'

I stared at him in surprise as I realised that he'd switched from English to a foreign language with a soft lyrical quality. I couldn't have named it, but I had no trouble translating it. I replied in the same tongue.

'Just a friend.'

'Clearly, from the way you had your arms around him. This isn't a game, Amara. Have you forgotten your training already?'

I shook my head in protest, but Nardo was too angry to notice my misery.

'Mariel will love this. She almost didn't let you go. She said you weren't old enough to appreciate the danger, let alone handle the responsibility. I argued in your favour. She wouldn't sign for you until the day before we left. You didn't know that did you? I thought you were ready, but clearly Mariel was right. You're too young. How bad is it? Have you compromised the whole operation or just yourself? Please tell me you haven't dragged Nell down with you.'

Fear almost suffocated me. 'Stop,' I gasped. I covered

my ears with my hands. 'It's not my fault. Nell's dead. She died in a car accident. I don't know how. I don't remember anything. Not you, or Nell, or Tor, or your stupid Confidentiality Decree.'

The colour drained from Nardo's face until he was whiter than a corpse. His anguished expression was more than I could bear. I bit my tongue and wished that I could go back in time and break the news again, more gently. Nardo stared at me. It was an eternity before he spoke. In a quiet voice he said, 'You're my sister. Amara Belle. For the love of Pietra! Have you really forgotten your name?'

I nodded miserably.

Nardo swallowed, then slowly he wiped the back of his hands across his eyes. 'Does anyone know about you? That boy, does he know how different you are?'

'No,' I lied instinctively.

'Good, that's one less person to deal with. Tell me everything, from the beginning. What happened? Where did you go after the accident? What have you been doing?' Nardo's voice cracked and he paused. He breathed deeply then continued with his questions. 'What happened to Nell's body?'

I didn't hear any more. Nardo wasn't the only one reeling with shock.

That's one less person to deal with.

What did he mean? Until I knew I wasn't giving anything away.

'This language we're speaking?' I asked. 'Is it Italian?'

Nardo shook his head. His expression was weary. 'You really don't remember, do you? We come from Pietra, a planet in a parallel universe to Earth. Do you understand, Amara? We're not from this world. We're aliens.'

SIXTEEN

Aliens! From the planet Pietra! I studied Nardo closely.
Was he teasing me? It didn't look like it. His dark brown
eyes were deadly serious.

'Why are we here?'

'To study humans and monitor their activities.'

'Why?'

Nardo sighed and ran a hand through his dark curls.
'It's complicated. The short answer is, we came because
of the *verboles*.'

The *verboles*? I knew the word, but my brain was
smothered in a dense fog and I couldn't find the
information I needed.

'Wormholes,' Nardo supplied me with the English
translation. 'A *verbole* is a passage through space and time.'

Of course it was. I remembered that now. 'So Pietra
and Earth, they're linked by a *verbole*?'

'They are linked by many *verboles*. There are two in
the United Kingdom, Europe has three and there are four
in the Americas. Africa and Asia have one each, and so
does Australasia. In Pietra there are also several *verboles*
that link us to small, uninhabited planets, only they're not

a problem.'

'But the ones that link Earth to Pietra, they are a problem?' I'd only just stopped myself from saying the ones that link *us* to Pietra. 'Is that how we got here, not by a spaceship but through a *verbole*?'

A ghost of a smile graced Nardo's lips. 'Sorry to disappoint you, Amara. There aren't any spaceships. Pietra doesn't have any. We came through the *verbole* in travel suits.' Nardo stared at me intently as if I might suddenly get my memory back. When I didn't say anything he continued. 'Pietra is very special. If humans discovered it, they would surely invade. In no time they'd spoil our planet, in the very same way they've spoiled Earth.'

'Have they spoiled Earth?'

'Amara!' My reaction startled and upset him. 'That's why we're here. It's a tragedy how badly humans have ruined Earth. It's overpopulated. They've plundered its natural resources. They've caused mass extinction of many animals and plants. They've also caused terrible pollution. The pollution is now so bad that the effects of it will ultimately result in this planet's destruction.'

I still didn't get why we were here. Wouldn't it have been safer to stay in Pietra and guard the wormholes from there?

'The first *verbole* in Pietra was discovered over

200 years ago,' Nardo continued. 'The planet that it linked us to was uninhabited, as were all the subsequent planets we visited when further *verboles* were discovered. Then, about a 100 years ago, we discovered Earth. It was a shock to find a planet that not only supported life, but in a form so similar to ours. Naturally, the discovery led to us conducting a study of humans.

The study concluded that Pietrans were physically the superior race but, and to our amazement, human technology was far more advanced. Our telekinetic skills had made us lazy. We'd neglected to progress in other areas. We started visiting Earth regularly. We've learned much from humans, especially from their mistakes. They have shown us how easy it is to ruin a planet through pollution and wars. Humans sought to build bigger and better, then fought each other to take control. We have concentrated on working together peacefully as one world. We've strived to ensure sustainability in all areas of our lives. As a result of our endeavours, Pietran technology is now far superior to Earth's. Our world is a better place to live in. The air is pure. The ground there is still rich in minerals and gems.

Another major step we took was to rid our planet of weapons. We unanimously decided on a 'no kill' rule. It's written into our constitution. In short, we have continued to come to Earth to study humans, but we also come to guard the *verboles*. There are Pietrans who live in this world solely to safeguard the security of ours. Humans are on a course of self-destruction. They'll continue to pollute and plunder Earth until eventually it will be unable to sustain life. The wiser humans know that already. But too few of those that govern will listen. When they finally face up to the facts it will be too late. Then, they will panic and look for somewhere else to colonise. It's imperative that they don't discover Pietra. If that happens, our studies lead us to believe that they will invade and take what we have.'

I sagged on my rock, numb from information overload. After his long speech Nardo lapsed into a tense silence. I counted the drips of water splashing on the floor. After a while I said, 'If Pietrans have learned from the mistakes of humans, and human technology has helped to advance Pietran technology, then don't we owe them something? We should offer them help and show them how to conserve their world.'

'No!' Nardo slammed his fist into the palm of his other hand. 'We've seen wars start when one country interferes with the affairs of another. We can't let them even *suspect* our existence. The risk would be too great.'

That seemed harsh and somewhat misguided. Pietra would only be offering advice not enforcing it. I wasn't going to argue the point now though. There were other things I needed to know first. 'So why am I here?'

'You're here to observe humans. You're a Watcher, the youngest Watcher ever. You were talent-spotted at school. You spent a month at the training centre being assessed. After a series of competitive tests you were one of fifteen applicants who were selected to be Watchers. There were over 700 candidates who'd applied for the job. Your official training lasted a further six months. Nell trained alongside you. She was to pose as a single mum and you were going to be her daughter. You were bound for Glasgow, where Nell was going to get a job and you were going to enrol at a college. Your Earth posting was for nine months.'

Relief welled inside me. I wasn't a criminal. I was a spy. A spy who wants to learn, not one who uses the information to harm.

'So Nell's not really my mother?'

'No.' Nardo shook his head and my heart leaped. That was such good news. 'Nell was Tor's wife. They only married last year. They were devoted to each other. Tor and I came here as Guards, to protect the entrance to the *verbole*.'

'I'm sorry about Nell.' It sounded both trite and insincere. I wanted to hug Nardo, but I was too shy. He didn't feel like my brother yet, more like an instructor.

'What about our mother? I'm surprised she let us come here together. It's a dangerous job, isn't it?'

Nardo's long fingers gripped my hand. 'We don't have a mother. I'm sorry, Amara. She died when you were a baby. It was completely unexpected. She went out jogging, early one morning, and she never came back. She suffered a heart attack. It seems that she had a rare, undiagnosed heart defect.'

'Oh!' For a second I couldn't breathe. I so badly wanted to meet my mother. Why did she have to be dead too?

Nardo let go of my hand. 'Father wasn't concerned about us coming here. Far from it! He was incredibly proud that we both were chosen. He's a *Polittica*, someone who governs and makes decisions.'

I was pleased I had a father and slightly surprised I hadn't wondered more about him. I shifted on the stone and wished there was more room, so I could get up and walk around. Over the weeks I'd imagined some pretty wild things about my past life but nothing like this. The relief that I wasn't into something *illegal* was huge. Not that the UK government might see it that way. Technically I'd entered their country illegally.

Nardo watched me, his expression inscrutable. 'Tell me about you,' he asked suddenly. 'Where have you been?'

'Well,' I said slowly, 'I don't recall arriving here,

obviously, or the accident. The first thing I remember was when I woke up in hospital. A man called Jeff Marshall and his son, Dan, rescued me. They pulled me from the car just before it exploded. They tried to save Nell too but they couldn't. Her seat belt was jammed. Nobody knew who we were. Nell was too badly burned to be identified and I was no help because I've got amnesia.'

'Did they run many tests on you at the hospital?'

'There were some X-rays, I think, to check that no bones were broken. After that it was just temperature and pulse.'

'No MRI scan?'

'No, I don't think so.' No one had mentioned giving me one of those.

'Good. Our brains are different to those of humans. We have an extra lobe, the *telechinatti*, that's responsible for the telekinesis. It's detectable on a human MRI scan, if you know what you're looking for. A doctor might spot it by accident, as it protrudes slightly from behind the *lobotti temporali*. What happened when they let you out of hospital?'

'It was awful at first. They wanted to put me in foster care. Then I got lucky. Jeff and his wife, Mia, offered me a place at Waterside, their school of music. They run summer courses, so there were lots of students staying and plenty of room for an extra one.'

'And the boy? Was that Dan?'

'Yes, he's a friend.'

'Your *amoretta*? Your boyfriend?' Nardo translated impatiently, when I gave him a blank look.

'No!' Not yet, but maybe now I knew who I was. People from different countries had relationships, why not those from a different planet?

'And he thinks you're just a regular girl?'

'Yes, but Holly knows I'm not. She's seen me do things with my mind.'

Nardo sat bolt upright.

'Who's Holly?'

'She's a girl… how old am I?'

'Sixteen human years. That's nearly nineteen in Pietran ones. I'm nineteen here. That's twenty-two back in Pietra.'

'Then she's the same age as me. She volunteers at the hospital. She brought me a drink but accidentally dropped it. When I caught it for her with my mind, she freaked out. She started to scream like I'd tried to kill her.' I smiled, even though it definitely hadn't been funny at the time. 'That was when I realised I wasn't like everyone else. Luckily the nurse in charge believed me when I said Holly caught the cup. I was very careful after that, until I ran into Holly again, at Waterside. She came for the summer

200

school. She spied on me until finally she caught me out for a second time. Then she got me kidnapped. I was locked in an empty house by her father and uncle, until I managed to escape.'

'What?' Nardo's voice rose to a shout. 'You should have told me this when we first met.'

'You didn't give me a chance. Besides, I didn't know if I could trust you. I've been having flashbacks, at least I think that's what they are, of a woman. She's smartly dressed with dark hair. In the flashbacks she's always telling me things. She gave me the impression that I shouldn't say too much.'

'That must be Carinna. She's a Trainer. Thank Pietra you remembered her.' Nardo ran a hand through his curls. 'Tell me about the kidnappers. I need to know everything.'

'There's not much to tell. Their names are Robert Jenkins, that's Holly's father, and Johnny Jenkins, her uncle. They locked me in a house. They were very interested in my telekinetic skills. They had plans to use me to make money. I think they wanted me to use my powers to steal things; they talked about a heist.'

'Money!' Nardo's eyes flashed with anger. 'There is no money on Pietra. There's no need for it. Everyone who can work does, so goods and services are given freely.'

There was no currency where I came from. That

201

explained a lot, I thought, inconsequentially. 'What happens if you can't or don't want to work?' I asked.

'Pietrans who genuinely can't work are looked after. Those that choose not to work, and their dependants, are left to starve. They soon change their minds and conform,' said Nardo abruptly.

Talk about black and white. There didn't seem room for shades of grey in Pietra.

Speaking slowly, to emphasise the point, Nardo said, 'Money! It's why it is imperative that humans do not discover Pietra. We have minerals and gems that they would kill to get their hands on.'

He stared at me for a while before asking, 'What happened after the kidnapping?'

Briefly, I told Nardo how I'd escaped from the house. I left out Dan's involvement and the car chase. I let him think that once I was free I'd contacted Dan and he'd driven me to Balochry, where he thought I was meeting Claudia. I'd explained that she was a girl I'd become friendly with on the summer school programme. It shocked me that I was such a natural liar, but my instincts were good. As soon as I'd finished speaking Nardo leaped up, almost banging his head on the dank rock ceiling.

'This is a serious breach of confidentiality. I've got to see Tor. Robert and Johnny have to be dealt with, immediately!'

Nardo had reached the mouth of the hollow. My heart raced as I scrambled after him. 'What do you mean? How will you *deal* with them?'

'Memory reassembly,' said Nardo, shortly.

'Memory reassembly?' Sweat beaded my hairline. 'You're going to alter their memories?'

'It's a chemical process. A small, colourless patch is stamped on the skin to induce a coma-like state. While the person sleeps the chemical wipes the memory of anything inexplicable. Holly, Robert and Johnny, they'll only remember who you are but nothing about your special skills or how they tried to kidnap you.'

'Is that legal?'

'In Pietra, yes, of course. Not that we have much call to use it. We live as a collective. Pietrans conform or suffer the consequences.'

We lived as a collective and suffered the consequences if we didn't conform. Really? So far I didn't like the things I was hearing about my homeland.

'Memory reassembly is harmless, usually,' Nardo continued. 'We've had a few casualties. Some people, who have an adverse reaction to the drug, lose all of their memories. There have also been a couple of deaths, mostly in elderly people. The shock of witnessing telekinetic activity often stresses the heart. The memory reassembly drug is harmless in itself, but it has very powerful effects on the system. When it's administered to the elderly it's often the final straw. Their heart gives out completely.'

Memory reassembly was harmless! No way. I didn't buy that. Not when there was any chance of dying from it and definitely not if it could accidentally erase all your memories. I was living that nightmare. Total memory loss was a terrifying experience. I wouldn't wish it on anyone.

'Come on. There's no time to waste.' Nardo was on the move. He pushed aside the fronds and stepped into the water. With long strides he waded up stream until he was clear of the rocks then he crossed the river and climbed out onto the opposite bank. I followed after him reluctantly. It was dangerous and slippery, but I struggled on and pretended not to see when he offered his hand to help me out of the water. I was shocked and still reeling over his casual approach to memory reassembly. I didn't care about Robert and Johnny. They were crooks. Kidnapping me at gunpoint was reprehensible and they had to be stopped from coming after me again. Holly was different. I didn't like her, but I didn't want to see her hurt. I'm not surprised she'd told her father about me. I'd scared her and got her into trouble at work. Then there was Dan. Fear clutched me. Dan was a totally innocent bystander. His only crime had been to help. I would not let Nardo reassemble Dan's memories.

SEVENTEEN

The ground became more rugged as we climbed. Nardo moved quickly as he forged a path through the scrubby bushes and tall trees. His eyes were everywhere, as if he was convinced that someone was following us. We saw no one but I was sweating with fear. What if Dan had followed us? What if Nardo caught him and reassembled his memory? We climbed on until my feet were stinging and I'd worn a hole through the sole of my left trainer. Nardo stopped suddenly and raised a hand, 'Can you feel it?'

I stood still and soaked up the incredible quiet. The Highlands were breathtakingly beautiful. The air was so pure. It filled me with a bubbling sense of anticipation. I felt as if I was on the edge of discovering something special.

'I feel funny.' I was having difficulty standing still. My feet wanted to keep moving.

'You're suffering from the effects of magnetic energy. We're really close to the *verbole* here.'

'Where are the Guards?'

'Around. You'll only see them if they want you to.'

My eyes raked the slopes above and below me. The only visible living thing was a bird of prey. It rode the thermals in slow circles above the trees.

'Come on,' said Nardo and he set off again.

He kept up the fast pace, even as he manoeuvred around a rocky outcrop. I climbed after him, gripping at the rock face with my hands. The ledge was narrow but the tingling feeling compelled me to hurry, even though the drop was steep enough to break my neck if I fell. On the other side of the rock, the path widened and then wound down to a small copse. Nardo hurried along it and disappeared into the trees. I followed until the path petered out. There was no sign of Nardo. I looked around uncertainly.

'Over here.' Nardo's head appeared on the other side of a tree.

The ground was veined with tree roots and scattered with old leaves. Apart from the occasional rustle, and the beat of bird wings, it was very quiet. I walked over, but when I got to the tree Nardo had gone again.

'Nardo?'

Unease needled my stomach. What was he playing at? Suddenly I longed for Waterside. I'd got what I'd come for. I knew who Amara was. Now I needed time – to work out what to do with my life, to decide who I wanted to be. Amara or Amber.

'Amara, up here.'

As I looked up, the strangest thing happened. A line appeared in the tree canopy, a thin vertical crack almost two metres high. I stared as it continued to widen. How was that possible? Suddenly, I realised that I was looking at a façade. That part of the canopy was nothing more than an image projected onto a door. The door slid open to reveal Nardo. He stood in the entrance hall of an incredible house with curved walls, built into an actual tree. He waved me up a staircase that had unfolded before him. The technology behind it was genius.

'Hurry up,' Nardo urged me.

My initial unease melted and left me with a burning desire to explore inside. I climbed the steps and when I reached the top Nardo put his hand on the wall. The staircase silently rose back up, folding into the floor like an escalator, as the door slid shut. Inside, the tree house was every bit as impressive as the exterior. A staircase flowed gracefully up to the second floor. At the top was a wide galleried landing, with lots of rooms hidden behind coloured doors. Downstairs, the entrance hall led into a large open living space. Nardo walked through it and I followed. The walls were the colour of butterscotch and tastefully interspersed with bright coloured panels in red, blue, green and orange. The room wasn't rectangular but followed the profile of the tree. Light filled the room, streaming in through a floor-to-ceiling window in the far wall. I was immediately drawn to it and stood to admire the panorama.

'This is amazing,' I said. 'You can see for miles but from the outside you'd never know there was anything here.'

Nardo's face was a blank wall as he stared back at me. 'So you don't remember the *portacasa*?'

'*Portacasa*.' I struggled to translate. 'Field camp? This feels pretty permanent.'

'Pietran technology,' said Nardo, with a hint of pride. 'Erected in hours.'

'Amara!' A bear of a man entered the room. His voice was deep and came from the depths of an enormous chest. Green eyes sparkled at me from under a thick fringe of sandy brown hair. He enveloped me in his muscular arms and hugged me tightly to him.

I hugged him back stiffly until he held me out and looked me up and down.

'You look well. You had us both worried when we couldn't make contact. Where's Nell? Is she missing me?' His booming laughter filled the room.

I stared at the ground, suddenly unable to face him. I felt like a traitor even though I hadn't done any wrong.

'Tor,' Nardo came to his side and laid a hand on his arm. 'I don't know how to break this to you. It's... it's not good. There was an accident – a fatal car crash. It happened the day that Nell and Amber arrived. I'm so sorry, but Nell... she's dead.'

Tor went rigid with his mouth open, his eyes wide and staring. For a split second no one moved. I couldn't even breathe. Then a low moan filled the room.

'Nooooo!' The word stretched out, as if Tor was falling from a cliff, and ended with a tortuous howl.

Tears rolled down my face. 'I'm sorry,' I whispered. 'I'm so sorry.'

The healthy tan seemed to leach from Tor's face. He stared straight through me and his eyes were full of pain. I wrapped my arms round my chest. I felt like a voyeur. I wished desperately that I could blot out Tor's anguish. When he suddenly crumpled, Nardo just caught him before he hit the floor.

'No!' Tor fought Nardo off. 'No! No! No!'

Nardo clutched him tightly and ignored the blows as they thundered down on his back. It was ages before Tor stopped struggling. Then he clung to Nardo. Tears streamed down his face. Unable to watch I turned away. I leaned with my head against the window and cried for a woman I wanted to remember but couldn't.

A long while later Nardo pressed a mug into my hands. It contained hot water and a slice of a bright green fruit that I didn't recognise. I cradled it to my chest and breathed in its sharp citrus smell. The warm steam on my face was a comfort. Tor slumped in a beanbag-like thing that had moulded into a chair when he sat down. He looked broken. His eyes were swollen to puffy slits and his skin was blotchy. He clutched a drink that Nardo had given him, and after a bit he said, in a croaky whisper, 'Tell me everything that happened to you.'

I recounted my story slowly, in a neutral tone. I made it clear that I hadn't formed any meaningful alliances when I'd gone to live at Waterside. As I spoke Tor reached inside his trouser pocket and pulled out a phone identical to mine only slightly larger. He sat with it in one hand, the fingers of his other poised over the keypad. The moment I stopped talking he asked for a detailed description of Robert, Johnny and Holly. I closed my eyes and drew pictures of them in my head. When I looked at Tor again he was entering the information I'd given him into his phone. His expression was intense as he swiftly pressed a sequence of on screen keys. With a satisfied sigh he rested the phone on the arm of the beanbag chair. He leaned forward and his bloodshot eyes searched my face. 'Again,' he said. 'From the beginning. Tell me what happened.'

This time, as I recounted what had happened, Tor questioned me relentlessly. He wanted every last detail of where I'd been, what I'd done and who with. I was careful to keep my lies consistent and met Tor's steady gaze with my own. All the while my heart was hammering. I was hot with fear in case I accidentally jeopardised the safety of Dan and all my new friends. When I reached the end of my account I fell silent. Tor exchanged a look with Nardo, who was by the window, a mug in one hand. As the silence spun around us I clamped my teeth together and fought the urge to open my mouth and add more detail. Something deep inside me, a remnant of my special training perhaps, was telling me not to overstate my case.

By the time Tor leaned forward, arching his fingertips together, my nerves were like shreds of torn paper. 'Amara,' he said softly, 'do you remember the Confidentiality Decree?'

'No.' My voice was barely a whisper.

'It's the most important part of our training. On an alien planet, every Guard and Watcher lives or dies by it. The decree forbids us to share information about our world. It also expressly forbids us to form any kind of relationship with humans. To do our job properly it is often necessary to become friendly with the people here on Earth. Friendly but *never* friends. Do you understand the difference?'

My throat tightened like an elastic band. I couldn't speak so I nodded my understanding.

'Under normal circumstances, anyone breaking the decree is sent home immediately where they are severely punished. These are not normal circumstances. If you have failed the decree you will be spared the consequences. It's important you tell me the truth. Have you broken the Confidentiality Decree?'

'No.' I let the word hang between us before I added, 'And yes.'

Tor raised an eyebrow, inviting me to explain.

'No, I haven't formed any deep friendships. But yes, I have made friends. Given my situation it would have been impossible not to. The Marshalls are lovely people. They took me in and gave me a home. It would have been unnatural if I hadn't formed any bonds with such a caring family.'

Tor said nothing, but I think my answer satisfied him because he picked up his phone and passed it to me. 'What do you think?' he asked.

My hands shook as I took it from him. On the screen was the computer-generated picture of a girl's face. 'That's Holly,' I gasped, stunned by the likeness.

'Any changes you'd make?'

I studied the picture again.

'Her nose is a little thinner and her left eye a fraction bigger than her right.' Funny how I'd only just realised that. 'But it's definitely her.'

Tor tapped on the screen.

'That's better.'

'And this?'

'Robert, only not so much grey in his hair. Yes, that's it. It's just like him. And you've got Johnny exactly.'

A satisfied smile curled the corners of Tor's mouth.

'Give me the address of your music school.'

'Why?'

'To locate Holly.'

I stopped with my mug halfway to my mouth as I thought about Dan, Mia, Jeff, Lucy, Josh and all the other students at Waterside. 'How will you get to Holly without anyone else knowing about it?'

'We're very good.'

I didn't doubt that, but Waterside was full of people and hadn't Nardo said that sometimes there were mistakes?

Tor studied me carefully. 'Do you have a problem with us going after Holly?'

'N-no, not at all,' I stammered.

'Good, because I'd send you home now if you did.'

For a wild second I thought that he meant Waterside

and my heart leaped for joy. Home was where I wanted to be, to make certain that Dan was out of the way when Tor and his Guards came for Holly. Then, in a rush, I realised Pietra was my real home and I was appalled. 'No! Don't send me back. There's no problem.'

Tor's eyes continued to bore into mine. 'You worry me – the amnesia – how can you possibly understand what's at stake?'

My chest went so tight I could hardly breathe. I wasn't ready to go back to Pietra. I wanted to see Dan and explain who I was. That much I owed him. But it was more than that. I wanted to talk to Dan, to share my feelings about this whole crazy situation and how I wasn't sure where I belonged any more. I trusted Dan. He wouldn't compromise this mission. He could keep a secret. And so could I.

'That's not fair. I've lived here for weeks without giving anything away. You can't blame me for Holly finding out about me. It was a combination of circumstance and bad luck. I'm part of a community. If I disappear back to Pietra now there'll be too many people who'll want to know where I've gone. Are you going to reassemble everyone's memories?'

I held my breath, not sure if I'd gone too far.

Tor stared at me for a long while. At last he said, 'You

make good points. But given your condition you can't continue with this mission. Nardo, work out a legend to cover for why Amara has been missing for so long without her family realising. Then falsify the human documents needed to back up that legend. You'll also need to arrange for Nell's body to be handed back…' He stopped abruptly.

'*Addessio*!' Nardo pulled a mobile from his pocket. He shot me a sympathetic smile before he left the room.

Addessio – immediately! My heart shattered into tiny pieces. Pietra wasn't giving me that warm fuzzy feeling that the thought of returning back home should. I didn't want to go there yet – or maybe ever.

EIGHTEEN

'We live and die by the Confidentiality Decree.'

Nardo and I were seated on high stools, facing each other across a counter in the *portacasa*'s smart, bright kitchen. It was practically the fiftieth time I'd heard it and the message was wearing a little thin. I'd lost my long-term memory, not my immediate one. Or was it my commitment that worried Nardo? Earlier that afternoon Tor, and a small group of Guards, had left to deal with Robert, Johnny and Holly. The moment we were alone Nardo had launched into a series of questions about my relationship with Dan. In his words, 'the boy he'd seen me hug, in Balochry'.

'We're friends,' I answered. 'I've already confessed to that. How was I to know, when I woke up and couldn't even recognise my own face, that I was an alien on this planet? Of course I was going to make new friends. I *needed* them. And here on Earth good friends hug each other all the time.'

Nardo tugged at his hair. 'Sorry, but I'm only doing my job. We hug in Pietra too. It's just, when I saw you together in Balochry, you seemed so much more intimate than friends would be.'

'I was scared. Dan was comforting me. Imagine how you'd feel if you were about to meet up with someone you couldn't remember, but they knew you. Dan even offered to come with me, for moral support.'

'Thank Pietra you didn't let him.'

'Yes, well…' I didn't add that the only reason I hadn't was because Nardo's texts had almost convinced me that I was a criminal.

'You're an *ambizia*, Amara,' Nardo smiled indulgently. 'That's why you were picked to come to Earth when you're still so young.'

'*Ambizia*?'

'A high flyer. Just as well. I've got to refresh the months of intensive training you undertook in the next sixty Earth minutes.'

'*Una andia*,' I answered. Bring it on.

Almost two hours later, when Nardo was still firing information at me, my head was reeling with overload.

'We're nearly done,' he said at last. 'Tell me the plan for tomorrow and then you can have the rest of the day off.'

Not that there was much of the day left. My stomach kept protesting that it was long past dinner time.

'I'll take the first train back to Edinburgh, then the bus from Edinburgh to Kirkgreen. I'll tell anyone who asks that I spent the night in a hotel with Claudia and her family.'

'Good. You won't have to stay at Waterside for long, a night at the most. By then I'll have contacted your social worker and claimed you as my missing sister.'

'Nicky will want documents to prove it,' I said.

'No problem,' said Nardo. 'I'm in the process of creating them. Your Italian passport was destroyed in the car accident, obviously, but I'll make sure there are computer records to prove your existence. This is our *legend* – we are Italians. The Pietran accent is similar and I've got personal knowledge of Italy. I spent a month there when I was training. There's a *verbole* not far from a place called Florence. I'll pose as an undergraduate, about to start at Edinburgh University in the autumn term. You and *mamma* came with me from Italy to see me settled in my student digs. You'd planned to tour Scotland before you returned home. We don't have a father and hardly any other relations either. That's why it's taken so long for anyone to realise that you were both missing. When I arrive at Waterside it will be easier if you don't remember me, so treat me like a stranger.'

That shouldn't be too difficult. Nardo still *was* a

stranger. It struck me that I should have asked him for paperwork, to prove that he had told me the truth. He could be anyone! There might not even be a Pietra. I looked around the modern kitchen, with its sleek lines and shiny gadgets. Nardo didn't need to prove himself. The technology here was far too advanced to be a product of Earth. This kitchen wouldn't have looked out of place on the bridge of a spaceship.

'So you come to Waterside, I pack up my things and we leave?'

'Yes, said Nardo. 'Take everything that you possess with you. We'll leave the Earth items here at the *portacasa*. You can't take anything back to Pietra unless it originally came from there. It's against the rules. We leave nothing on Earth but our footprints, we take nothing away with us but memories and, of course, our findings.'

Except in my case, the memories of my previous life would be left behind too. I swallowed back a wave of sadness. I liked it here. I'd made friends. It felt too soon to start again somewhere new, especially somewhere as regimented as Pietra sounded. Nardo noticed my distress. He reached across the counter and squeezed my hand. 'It'll be easier this time. At least in Pietra you'll be with people who know and love you.'

I could never let on that there were people who cared

for me here. 'Tell me about my life in Pietra.'

Nardo looked pleased. 'I hoped you'd ask me that. Tor warned me not to give you too much information about your past. He said to let you set the pace. It's just a shame that I don't have the *graphoria* with me. We're not allowed to bring any personal stuff with us from Pietra, in case we're compromised.'

'*Graphoria*, is that like a camera?'

'It's much more realistic that an ordinary Earth camera. A *graphoria* projects moving images in three dimensions. It also recalls smell and temperature. It makes you feel like you're witnessing the recorded event at first hand. So what do you want to know about?'

Where to start? I had more questions than stars in the night sky. 'Tell me about Amara. What do I do in my spare time?'

'You're very sporty, you love swimming and sailing and you play *tennita*. You're on the junior team at the local club. You're also musical. You play *fluetto* for the Rosso Youth Orchestra. *Rosso Tiree*, Red Three is the region where we live.'

I played *fluetto*. Suddenly my favourite song, the one that I couldn't get out of my head, was running through my head. 'I can play this, can't I? What's it called?' I hummed some of the tune.

Nardo's eyes grew large, '"*Amorra Mi*" !' he exclaimed. 'You remembered!'

'"My Love",' I translated. I was childishly pleased that I'd known the tune was a love song. It gave me hope that more of my memory would return. 'I can play it on the *fluetto*, or flute, an Earth instrument that's similar.'

Nardo was watching me as if he was hoping for more. I risked a guess. 'Did I compose it?'

He answered my question with a sad smile. 'Marn composed it. Do you remember him?'

I shook my head.

'He's a very good friend. He's the same age as me. I've known him since we were *bambinetts*. He plays *fluetto* with the Rosso Youth Orchestra, like you do. Marn had hoped to become a professional musician but he wasn't allowed, he was too intelligent, so instead he chose to become a Guard.'

I was shocked and disappointed for Marn, who clearly had a great musical talent. 'Musicians are intelligent too. Who wouldn't let him become one? Was it his parents?'

'It's the way we live. Our constitution decrees that every citizen must work, unless they are too old or too infirm. It's vital, for the good of Pietra, that people are channelled into the right career. Many intelligent people are creative, but not all creative people are intelligent.

Think of the waste to our society if a highly intelligent person was allowed to do a creative or menial job. It's Marn's duty to pick a career that only clever people can do. He didn't have to be a Guard. He could have trained for other jobs, such as a doctor or a scientist. Marn's adventurous and he loves to travel. When he was told that he couldn't become a musician he knew, immediately, that he wanted to train as a Guard. He passed the entry requirements at the same time as me. We trained together.'

'Guards are highly intelligent?' I didn't doubt either Marn or Nardo's credentials, I was just surprised that being a Guard was considered as prestigious as becoming a doctor.

Nardo sat taller. 'Yes, we have to be. We have great responsibility. The security of Pietra is in our hands.'

Pietrans were paranoid if you asked me. They'd got humans totally wrong. Yes, there were bad ones, like Johnny and Robert, but there were far more good ones like Dan, Mia and Jeff. I wasn't going to argue with Nardo. I didn't want him to question my loyalty when I was unsure of it myself. I changed the subject quickly. 'It's a beautiful song.'

'Yes.' Nardo's eyes misted over. 'It came from the heart. Marn wrote it as a gift for his *amoretta*. He gave it to her on her sixteenth birthday.'

'Wow! That's some present. She must be a very special girl.'

'She is,' said Nardo softly. 'I wish you could remember her.' A cloud seemed to pass over his face, as if he was struggling to tell me something. It left me wondering. Had Nardo loved Marn's girlfriend too? My suspicion was strengthened when Nardo said abruptly, 'Let's have a drink.' He hopped off the stool. 'I'll make some *limonge*. Hot or cold?'

'Hot, please.' I was dying to see some of the kitchen gadgets in action.

Nardo opened a cupboard and brought out mugs. He removed two round stones from a drawer and placed one inside each mug. He carried the mugs across to the stainless steel sink and swiped his hand across the single tap, twice. Water poured from the tap into the first mug. When it was full the tap automatically directed the jet into the second mug, then stopped when it was full. Nardo added thick slices of a green fruit. He cut them with a thin wire that he controlled with his mind. A minute later steam curled from the mugs. He used his mind to remove the stones and left them on the worktop, where they continued to hiss and steam. There was no damage to the worktop though. The whole process took less than a minute. I hid my amazement as Nardo passed me the drink.

'I'll prepare dinner soon,' he said. 'It's not from scratch, I'm afraid. When we're in the field we rely heavily on Earth cubes. They're easier to transport and to store. They're not bad though. They're nutritious and they satisfy.'

'How does all this stuff get here?' I waved my hand around the room. 'Is it easy to transport through the wormhole, I mean *verbole*?'

'It's transported in capsules. They're egg-shaped and they have landing legs, or stabilisers, that eject on impact. They stand about a metre high. We're working on a design that carries people, but it's not proving very comfortable and, unfortunately, it doubles the travelling time.' Nardo took a long swig of his drink. As he put his mug down my stomach grumbled with hunger.

I felt my face colour up, but Nardo thought it was funny.

'Hungry?' he asked.

'Starving. I had a grilled chicken sandwich for lunch, but I was too nervous to eat much of it.'

'Chicken?' Nardo's face darkened. 'Have you been eating meat?'

'Yes. Why, am I a vegetarian?'

'By the love of Pietra! Have you learned nothing this afternoon? We went through the rules several times. Rule *dua*, we will not intentionally kill. That means *everything*. We're vegetarians. The only animal products we consume are those that can be taken without harming the animal. Food such as unfertilised eggs and milk. We also use wool. Once an animal dies, we're allowed to use its skin. But we never eat flesh.'

My stomach curled and tightened into a knot. I clutched my mug and wished Nardo would stop staring at me like I was some kind of puppy-eating monster. I hadn't eaten meat intentionally. At first I hadn't even known what it was. Nardo stood up. 'The sooner we get you home the better. Earth is ruining you.'

He moved around the kitchen, putting together strange, coloured cubes for our meal. It was too late for me. I'd lost my appetite again. Darkness fell outside but the room remained bathed in a soft white glow. I looked about me until I sourced the light to a number of small transparent balls, positioned around the room. I hadn't seen anything like them before.

'What are they?' I asked, before I could stop myself.

'*Illuminetta*. They're solar-powered lamps,' Nardo explained. 'They're totally renewable and non-polluting.'

I thought of my mobile phone and how that glowed

in the daylight. It had to be solar powered too. A million questions buzzed in my head like honey-drunk bees, but I didn't know where to start so ate in silence. Nardo seemed thoughtful and occasionally I'd catch him watching me. We finished the meal with a dark brown cube that had a rich chocolaty taste. I was so full I couldn't be bothered to move. Nardo began to clear up. He filled the sink with water, several large heat stones and a clear, purple-coloured liquid that I guessed was a cleaning agent. I reached for his plate to carry it with mine to the sink, but somehow it slipped out of my grasp.

'Oops!' My heart skipped, but instead of smashing on the floor the plate rose up and hovered in front of me. I glanced at Nardo, nonchalantly leaning up against the counter. His eyes travelled to the plate and then back to me. I smiled my thanks and reached out with my mind to take it from him. Nardo blocked me. I nudged his mind again, a friendly enquiry, but still Nardo refused to let go of the plate. Then all at once something clicked into place. I seized my plate and sent it flying into the air. Nardo pulled himself up straight. With a wicked grin he sent his plate across the room to the washing up bowl. I was determined not to be beaten and spun my plate to make it go faster. Adrenalin surged through me as I overtook Nardo then held the plate in front of his, to deliberately slow him down.

Nardo laughed and retaliated by making his plate side-step mine. When he'd overtaken me he stopped his plate abruptly. It hovered in the air and mine almost ran into the back of it. I spluttered with laughter. I took evasive action, by sending my plate down to dive under his. In the lead now, I spun my plate towards the washing up bowl and dropped it into the water with a satisfying splash.

'Beat you!' I couldn't resist saying.

Nardo was laughing so hard he could hardly stand up. Somehow he managed to guide his plate into the washing up bowl. He made an even bigger splash than I had. 'You remember?' he choked out.

'Yes, no, I ...' Did I remember? Something hovered on the edge of my consciousness. 'It's a game we play?'

'Right! It was something we did to...' Suddenly Nardo was serious again. 'Do you remember Mariel?'

I shook my head. Her name meant nothing, except that earlier Nardo had mentioned that I needed her permission to come on this mission to Earth.

'Who is she?'

His eyes hardened. 'Our stepmother.'

'Oh!' I was surprised by his change of mood. 'Don't we like her?'

'Not much.'

'So the plate thing, that has something to do with her?'

'We do it to wind her up.' Nardo smiled bitterly. 'It drives her mad.'

As he spoke a picture was forming in my head of a tall, beautiful woman in a deep blue dress that clung to her curvaceous figure. Her long blonde hair was piled on top of her head and laced through with glittering jewels. She was on a riverbank and smiling at someone I couldn't quite see. The image was so strong that I could feel the sun burning my face and smell the cool blue water. A crowd had gathered behind me and as I turned I was greeted with a sea of smiling faces. All I could feel though, was an acute sadness that gnawed away at my insides. The image died and it was several minutes before the ache left me.

'Mariel... has she got long blonde hair? Was there a time down by the river, with a crowd of people?' My voice petered out as I struggled to control my emotions.

Nardo stared at me. I knew he was hoping that I'd remember more. As the silence lengthened he said, 'That was the day she married our father.'

Our father. His tone was so formal. 'Don't we get on with him either?' I asked.

'Of course we do. He loves us more than anything, except her of course.'

I waited for Nardo to tell me more about our father

but he seemed lost in his own thoughts. Eventually, he said in a matter-of-fact way, 'Things changed when father met Mariel, but at least she makes him happy.'

Not us though! The implication was clear. Was that the reason I'd become a Watcher? To escape from my home?

'You remembered plate racing!' said Nardo, changing the subject. 'Now I know you're my Amara and not an imposter.'

He leaned forward and flicked me playfully on the nose with his finger.

'Get off,' I retaliated, smacking his hand away.

'Yep!' said Nardo smugly. 'It's you.'

We laughed together and suddenly a small part of the blackness snuffing out my past dissolved. It wasn't much but it felt good. Unfortunately, Nardo went and spoiled the moment. 'You'll need more of these,' he said. He pulled a slim, cylindrical object from his pocket.

'What is it?' I put out my hand curiously, then recoiled as he answered, 'Memory reassembly patches. It's okay! This is just the applicator.'

Nardo mistook my revulsion for fear. He rolled the device in his hand. 'It works like a stamp. You put the end against a bare patch of skin – the neck works best – then press down once to release a patch. The patches are clear and they dissolve. There's no trace of chemicals, or anything. Clever, isn't it?'

'Hmm,' I said non-committally.

'See the gauge on the bottom?' Nardo turned the applicator upside down. 'It shows how many patches are left. You get 50 per applicator. This one's full. Here, you can have it.'

'Don't you need it?' I asked, reluctant to take it from him.

'I've got two and there are plenty more here in the store. Don't be shy about using it. Remember, the safety of our world…'

'Is in my hands,' I finished.

'That's it!' The hollow ring to my words were lost in Nardo's delight. 'You're going to be fine! You had me worried earlier over the meat. You didn't seem to have grasped the underlying principles of our life. I seriously considered asking Tor to send you home immediately. It would have been complicated, but we can perform mass memory reassembly by releasing an airborne chemical. We don't like doing it, as it's not as safe as using the patches. In trials, one in a hundred people ends up losing all their memories. But you can do this, can't you Amara? You'll manage the exit plan without compromising us?'

'Yes, of course.' It wasn't a lie. I wouldn't compromise anyone, especially Dan and my Waterside friends.

As the evening wore on and Tor didn't return I grew more anxious. What if something had gone wrong? Had Tor and the Guards ended up dealing with more people than they'd intended to? What if they'd been forced to perform a mass memory reassembly? What if it had failed, leaving Dan with his memories wiped? The thought left me breathless.

NINETEEN

I asked Nardo if I could hide away just before the Guards changed shifts. I didn't want the ordeal of meeting a bunch of people who knew me but whom I couldn't remember. Nardo took me upstairs to a large walk-in store cupboard.

'You can sit in here. It won't be for long,' he reassured me. 'As soon as the night shift have gone to work there'll be a free bedroom for you.' He'd gone on to explain that there were two teams of Guards. 'Tor's in charge of the day team, I'm his second in command. Leesa is in charge of the Night Guards. Her second is Ando. The bedrooms sleep two guards and are shared by both shifts. You can sleep in mine and Tor's room once Leesa and Ando have gone to work.'

In one day I'd been kidnapped, held prisoner, escaped twice and discovered the truth of my identity. I was physically and emotionally shattered, but sleep was the furthest thing from my mind. I'd have been happy to spend the night in the store cupboard. Nardo had given me a hand-held *illuminetta* and one of the beanbag chairs. It was cosy and the chair was very comfortable. I settled down and immediately thought about Dan. The way we'd parted in Balochry still troubled me. I wanted to explain to him why I'd pushed him away. I considered ringing him, but was too scared to in case anyone heard me. I could send a text, though. Then Dan would know I was safe and thinking about him. I tapped his number out on my phone keypad. Now, what should I say?

Words formed in my mind but each time I committed them to the screen they sounded all wrong. I deleted message after message until finally I settled for,

Miss you. Back tomorrow. Ax

It wasn't much but it would have to do. I pressed the send button and watched the lengthening blue line track the progress of my text. As the line and message finally disappeared I gripped the mobile. Would Dan text me back? My breath quickened as the mobile vibrated. I'd got an incoming message. Warmth spread through me. Dan had been waiting for me to call. Then, as I glanced at the screen, my hopes were dashed. My own message flashed on the screen along with a red line and two dots, to indicate that it had failed to send. I should have seen that coming. I was hiding in a cupboard deep in the Highlands. Of course I wouldn't get a signal. I bit back my disappointment and put the phone away.

A long while later Nardo came and moved me to the

room he shared with Tor. It was bare and impersonal, with bunk beds and a small wardrobe. There was a square window and, like the ones downstairs, it didn't have curtains – as night fell the glass darkened with it.

'The top bunk's mine,' said Nardo. He handed me a clean blanket. 'The bathroom is the first door on the right. I'll wake you at six so that we can be out of here before everyone else gets up. Sleep well, Amara.'

I doubted I'd sleep at all. There was too much going on in my head. I'd hoped that when I learned my identity I'd have choices: to either go back to my old life, or to continue with my new one. But I was a Pietran and, from everything I'd learned so far, a Pietran's choices were limited. It wasn't fair. I liked being Amber. I wasn't convinced that I'd like being Amara. Granted, she sounded amazing. She was the youngest Watcher ever. She was clever, competent and brave. At sixteen she'd travelled a universe to spy on humans. She hadn't come to Earth to make friends or meet a cute boy.

Was that the real Amara, though? What if she'd had an ulterior motive? Her home life didn't sound a bundle of fun. Say she hadn't really wanted to be a Watcher, but saw it as a chance to escape. What then? The more I thought about it the more I wondered. The Confidentiality Decree bothered me too. Nardo couldn't have made its importance any clearer. We lived and died by it! Tor had been sympathetic to my situation. He recognised that I couldn't break rules when I didn't remember them. His words played back in my head, *'These are not normal circumstances. If you have failed the decree you will be spared the consequences. It's important you tell me the truth. Have you broken the Confidentiality Decree?'*

Only I hadn't told him the truth. I'd lied to save Dan. I didn't regret it. There was no way I'd put Dan, or any of my close friends, through memory reassembly. It didn't matter how small the risks were. I wasn't prepared to take them. Tor or Nardo would never understand how strongly I felt about this. How could they? They hadn't lost their memories.

I went along to the bathroom. It had a shower and a people drier, a metal plate in the ceiling with holes that blew warm air over you. It was a luxury that I'd missed. Nardo had even thought to find me some clean clothes from the emergency pool, a pair of khaki coloured jeans, a green T-shirt and a dark green hoodie. The clothes were unique. None of the Guards wore uniform.

'Uniforms are for armies,' Nardo told me with a shiver. 'In Pietra no two outfits are the same. Here in the field things are slightly different though. Our clothes have to be similar as Guards need to blend in with the scenery.'

I was too hot in bed and the blanket stuck to me like cling wrap. I stretched out my feet to search for a cool spot. There wasn't one. I kicked the blanket off but I still couldn't get comfortable. I lay awake for ages while a million thoughts scrambled for a space in my mind. A million thoughts that all led back to the same place. Dan. I didn't want to return to Pietra. I wanted to stay here and get to know him properly.

I slept eventually, in that awful, wide-awake way where your brain doesn't shut down. My thoughts were muddled up with my dreams and I knew I'd be shattered, come the morning. When there was activity outside my room, terse whispers and the slow tread of feet coming up the stairs, I woke immediately.

'Careful, keep his arm up. He's still losing blood.'

'Does Milo know?'

'Yes, he came back ahead of us to get the *cura casa* ready.'

Cura casa. That meant medical room. Someone was hurt. I climbed off the bunk, tiptoed to the door and silently opened it. Tiny lights illuminated the stairs. They reminded me of landing lines on a runway. In the semi-darkness I saw two men carrying a third up the stairs. Nardo and Tor brought up the rear.

'He took us by surprise,' said Tor wearily. He ran a

hand over his forehead. 'He must have been following Amara for ages. Luckily we caught him before he got back to Balochry. He told us he'd called the police. He was lying. We checked his mobile afterwards. We guessed he'd be armed, but the weapon took us all by surprise. It's one thing to see a gun on the *graphoria* during training, but when you're staring into the barrel of a real one... By the love of Pietra, it was surreal!' There was a tremble in Tor's voice. 'Amara's been much braver than we realised. Hern screamed when the bullet hit him... it was... I thought he'd been killed. Why didn't I stop it? I can bend metal. I could have distorted the barrel of the gun so that the bullet hit the ground. There was no time to react, though. Johnny was quick. He shot before we realised that he wasn't bluffing. It was total chaos.'

I held my breath, silently pulling the door shut, as the injured man was carried past. When I reopened it, just a crack, Nardo and Tor were standing outside.

'You did everything you could,' said Nardo quietly. 'Look how quickly you got Hern back here. He'll be fine. He's young and he's tough.'

'It's a bad wound. The bullet only just missed a main artery. He's lost a lot of blood. I wish we could get him home, but he's not strong enough to make the journey.'

'Milo will see him right. He's an *ambizia medicio*.'

'I don't doubt Milo's capabilities. That's why he's here, but he doesn't have the same medical facilities available to him as he would in Pietra.'

The injured man was carried into a room at the end of the corridor. Nardo and Tor went in and closed the door. I stepped out of my room with the intention of continuing my eavesdropping – well, I am a Watcher, but Tor and Nardo came straight back into the corridor. Silently I retreated.

'Where's Johnny now?' asked Nardo.

Tor sighed heavily. 'No one knows. He took off into the mountains. I sent six Guards after him. I couldn't spare any more. We're already five down, that's Hern and the four it took to carry Robert back to town. He's sleeping like a baby. The Guards left him a short way off the tourist path with an empty bottle of spirits. He'll feel like he has a major hangover when he wakes.'

Tor and Nardo laughed together and I had to bite my lip not to shout at them. Memory reassembly just wasn't funny.

'What now?' Nardo's voice grew louder as he walked my way.

'I need your help to find Johnny. We can't let him go. He's seen too much. When he ran off, he was shouting about the government, aliens and a conspiracy theory.'

At once I stepped out of the room. 'I'll help too.'

Nardo's face was full of approval but Tor said firmly, 'No. It's too risky.'

'Why?'

'You should know why.'

'You don't trust me?'

'I'd have sent you home by now if I didn't trust you, but you've lost your memory. Mess this up and you can wave goodbye to our world. You'll stay here.'

There was a cold edge to his voice that I didn't deserve. I felt awkward, like a little girl that's been caught in the act of dressing up in adult clothes. Tor swept down the stairs. Nardo shot me an apologetic smile as he hurried after him. Minutes later I heard the front door slide open and then shut again. Silence followed. My breath stuck in my throat. It was stupid, but I was disappointed that Nardo hadn't come back to see me before he left. He was my brother after all. It reinforced how little I remembered of him. The room seemed suddenly darker especially in the corners where the shadows lay thick and black. The minutes crept by, one slow second at a time. I was going mad waiting and not knowing what was going on. Eventually, for something to do, I got up and went downstairs for a drink. The kitchen was in darkness. For few futile moments I searched for a light switch, before I realised that all I had to do was to wave my hand in front of the *illuminetta* to switch them on. I poured myself a mug of water and stood at the window with it. It was unnaturally quiet. There were no weird gurgling noises, the signature tune of an Earth hot water system, or the hum that accompanies electrical devices. The silence made me homesick for Waterside. I rested my head against the window and enjoyed the cool touch of glass on my burning forehead. Outside a light flickered through the trees. I waited for Tor, Nardo, or another Guard to appear. No one did. My heart beat too quickly in my chest. It made me breathless. Who exactly was creeping around outside?

The copse of trees remained blacker than pitch. I continued to stare out of the window. There was nothing to see and gradually my heart slowed. I'd been mistaken. I gave a shaky laugh, embarrassed by my neurosis. I drained my mug of water and as I poured myself another one, a thought skewered me to the spot. What would happen when Tor caught Johnny? Would he reveal that Dan had been with me during the car chase and knew about my special skills? Tor and Nardo would be furious with me. They'd see me as a traitor for not telling them about Dan. I'd be sent back to Pietra in disgrace, instead of the victim of a terrible accident. And what of Dan? I didn't care what they did to me. But I cared about Dan.

Tor had only ordered Amara to stay put. But I was Amber too and, as Amber, I had to find Johnny before anyone else did. I left my mug on the counter and made my way to the front door. Another unwelcome thought crash-landed in my head. How would I stop Johnny from giving Dan away? Somehow I didn't think that appealing to his better nature would work. *Go on*, I goaded myself, *admit it*. I was going to use the memory drug on him. The thought appalled me. But what choice did I have?

TWENTY

The first pale streaks of dawn nudged at the night sky as I left the *portacasa*. I didn't have a clue where to start looking for Johnny, but I guessed he would head for town, so I went in that direction. I hadn't gone far, just to the edge of the copse of trees, when I had a sudden, inexplicable urge to turn around and go the opposite way. I couldn't explain it but the desire was too strong to be ignored. The fresh morning air was potent and it made my head reel. Soon, I was very dizzy. I let my feet take control and they hurried me up a stony track. The surrounding land was deserted, but I knew I wasn't the only person out here looking for Johnny. The thought spurred me on. A mountain rose before me, grey and shadowy in the half-light. It was so cold. My eyes hazed with tears until I couldn't see anything and had to stop climbing. Even then my legs didn't want to stand still and I found myself jogging on the spot. I rubbed my eyes with my fists. That was better. Now I could see more clearly. Suddenly, I was aware of something moving on the slope above me. I ducked down beside a bush. A tall, athletic figure moved stealthily across the mountain. My jaw literally dropped and my mouth opened. No. It couldn't be.

'Dan, you idiot,' I silently cursed him. I was furious and deliriously happy at the same time. My Dan, always the hero! He'd cared enough about my safety to follow me for a second time. Oh Dan, if only you knew of the danger you'd put yourself in. I broke into a run, moving as silently as possible over the stone-strewn ground, until I stumbled. Stones sprayed down the slope, clattering loudly as they gathered speed. I fought to regain my balance and when I looked up again Dan had vanished. Where had he gone? I stared across the slope but there was nowhere to hide. Had I imagined seeing Dan? If I was honest I wasn't feeling great. My head was still spinning. I wanted to lie down but my feet were wired and they wouldn't stop moving. They propelled me forward until in desperation I planted them wide. I bent over and put my hands on my knees in an attempt to physically anchor myself to the ground. Any minute now I was going to be sick.

There was a sharp click then something hard was pressed between my shoulder blades.

'Don't move,' growled Johnny softly.

When someone has a gun to your back it's probably a good idea to follow instructions, but I was beyond caring about my safety. Anger chased away my earlier nausea.

I moved at the speed of lightning and crushed my heel into Johnny's foot. He yelped. I felt the gun waver. I spun round to knee him in the groin. Then I reached out and took hold of the gun with my mind. Johnny knew that trick and was ready for me. His grip on the gun was so solid there was no way I could wrestle it from him. I remembered what I'd overheard Tor say, how he could shape things with his mind, and wondered if I could do that too. Again my mind reached for the barrel of the gun.

Bend.

Nothing! I could feel it in my mental grasp but the metal wouldn't yield.

Bend.

I created a stronger picture in my head and imagined the gun distorting, until the barrel of the gun pointed at the ground. My head ached with the effort of maintaining the image. I forced myself to stayed focused, until finally I admitted that it wasn't going to work. I could move things without touching them but I couldn't alter their shape.

Johnny pushed the gun against my back. He edged round me until we were face to face. In one quick movement he gripped my arm and transferred the gun to the side of my head. A cruel smile played on his lips. 'Don't even think about the mind stuff. Try it and I'll shoot.'

'Okay,' I gasped.

I dropped my eyes as if defeated.

'Walk,' he said. He pressed the gun to my skin in a warning.

'Where are we going? What do you want?' I asked.

'Gold, lassie. That's what you are.'

His rank breath made me gag. I forced myself to ignore it, to concentrate on escaping instead. Then I had an idea. I just needed a stone to make it work. I searched the ground until I located one that was small and round as a pea. Johnny began to mutter. At first I wasn't sure if he was talking to me, or himself.

'This whole thing is much bigger than I thought. You're not alone. There's a colony of you living up here in the mountains. Aliens, that's what you are! Where's your spaceship then? Show me. Show me, now. People need to know about this. Forget the police. I'll go to the papers first. Yes! That's what I'll do. The nationals will pay a fortune for my story. I'll need photos of your ship and I'll take you along as proof. I'll go for an exclusive. It's got to be worth six figures at least.' His voice rose with excitement. 'It'll be so much easier than our original plan of getting you to steal for us. And better still it'll be legal! I won't have to keep looking over my shoulder for the police. I've always wanted a yacht, I can have one now. I'm going to sail to the Caribbean, or maybe I'll get a condo in Vegas. Or both!'

I focused on the stone and lifted it with my mind. I watched it, out of the corner of my eye, until it was the same height as the gun. My head spun and I couldn't focus properly to line up the stone with the gun's barrel. I cursed silently as I overshot, but eventually I had the stone in the right place. It was a perfect fit. All I had to do now was to slide it forward and jam it in the gun's barrel.

The crack of gunfire made me shriek. My stone exploded and fell to the ground in a thousand tiny pieces. Johnny grabbed me by the collar. He pressed the gun's barrel under my chin. 'No tricks,' he yelled. 'The next bullet's yours. Now walk.'

He yanked my arm so high up my back I thought it might snap in two. I moved reluctantly in the direction he was shoving me. I felt weird and a pressure was building in my head. I dragged my feet and stones flew up from my shoes. Johnny yanked my arm higher. 'Move it,' he yelled, as he stumbled against me. 'Faster.'

My head hurt so badly. I wanted to lie down in the dew-splattered grass until the pain had gone.

'Stop that!' Johnny's mouth was right by my ear. His voice sounded distant, like he was shouting at me from the top of the mountain. I don't know why but it made me laugh.

'I said, stop it.'

'Stop what?' My words came out slurred.

'You're messing with my head.'

'You're messing with mine.' I felt so light-headed it made me giggle. I kept remembering things, snippets of conversation, useless facts, something important that Nardo had told me about this very mountainside – but my thoughts were like dreams and they constantly shifted and drifted out of reach. What did it matter, anyway? I didn't care any more. Everything was too weird. I tripped over my feet and bit my tongue, tasted the blood in my mouth, and then I remembered the something important.

Magnetic energy. The wormhole was surrounded by it. At once everything fell into place. It was why I felt so bad, why Johnny had blamed me for messing with his head. We were both suffering from the effects of magnetic energy. The *verbole* had to be very close. I stopped and stared around, searching for... for what? I didn't know what I was looking for. A hole, I guess. A big one if people could travel through it. But there my imagination stopped. Through the fog in my brain a voice struggled to make itself heard. Johnny didn't know about Pietra. He mustn't find out about it.

'Move it.'

The cool metal of the gun soothed the ache in my

head, but I hated the way Johnny was leaning on me. He was also very heavy.

'Careful,' I said as I felt my knees buckle.

'Move,' Johnny slurred. He grabbed my hair and dragged me along by it. My scalp was on fire but the pain sharpened my senses. I had to get a memory patch on him. I had an applicator. Nardo had given me one. I slid my hand into my pocket and located it with my fingers. It didn't repulse me like it had earlier. With a gun to my head it felt like I was holding the hand of a trusted friend.

'Now what are you up to?' Johnny let go of my hair and snatched savagely at my arm. As he pulled my hand out of my pocket I only just managed to let go of the applicator. It dropped back into my pocket. Johnny pinned both arms to my sides and held me in a bear hug. I could barely move, so I brought my head back and smashed it against his chin. At the same time I stamped on his foot.

'You bitch! You nearly broke my nose.' He squeezed me until I couldn't breathe. 'Do that again and I'll shoot,' he snarled.

I laughed. 'Go on, then. I'll be really useful to you dead.'

Johnny snorted with anger, then yanked my arm up my back. His grip was solid. I whimpered in pain.

'Shut up.' He lurched and dragged me forward with

him. I lashed out with my foot and kicked his kneecap.

'Stop it, bitch.' His fingers bit into my arms. He stumbled on, pulling me with him. The ground grew steeper, but it didn't slow him down. In my confused state it took me a while to realise that Johnny couldn't have stopped even if he'd wanted to. An unseen force had taken hold of both of us. It was like being caught up in a tornado. My hair whirled over my face and blinded me in a haze of chestnut. Another step and the ground suddenly disappeared. As Johnny and I fell, dropping like stones in a well, the temperature plummeted. The light was instantly devoured by a darkness even deeper than black. Stupid thoughts crossed my mind. I was glad I'd fallen feet first. If I'd eaten I'd be throwing up by now. Why couldn't it be Dan's arms around me instead of Johnny's?

Dan. I could see him clearly. Those blue eyes that crinkled when he laughed. The cute way he'd raise an eyebrow. His hair, tousled even when he'd just combed it. I saw his long fingers dancing on the sax keys, while his body swayed in time with the music. I felt his tanned arm pressing against me when we sailed together. His soft lips as they'd brushed mine when he'd tried to kiss me. Heat flooded my face. For all the things I could have regretted, there was only one I was truly sorry for.

I'd turned away when he'd kissed me.

TWENTY-ONE

We had to be travelling through the wormhole. I must have done it before but I was terrified. My thoughts tumbled with me, black and empty as the void I was spinning through. I didn't want to go back to Pietra yet. I definitely didn't want to arrive there with Johnny's arms wrapped around me, like we were an item. I tried to shake him off but it was impossible. A force was squeezing the life out of me. It rendered me immobile and I couldn't even blink. My eyes were fixed in a wide-open state, like a doll with a scary painted face. I completely lost all sense of direction. Up, down, who cared? It was too black to see anyway. Time passed, seconds, minutes, hours, I really didn't know. The journey seemed endless.

At some point I sensed we were slowing. A while later tendrils of light snaked towards us. They grew slowly stronger until suddenly we burst from absolute black into a dazzling bright light. We flew into the light, then slammed into the ground. Johnny's arms went limp, setting me free. I rolled away from him, gasping for breath. The air had gone and my lungs were stuck together. There was a gurgling sound, my chest burned, and the air rushed in again. I lay on my back and looked up at the sky. Too bright! Wincing, I shielded my eyes with a hand. It felt like I'd been wearing sunglasses and they'd suddenly been ripped away. I wanted to stay here until the world stopped spinning, but instinct screamed at me to move. I sat up carefully and looked about. I was on the side of a mountain. At first glance it was almost identical to the one I'd come from. But when I looked at it more closely I could see it wasn't the same. If Pietra was a photo then Earth was a smudged copy. Everything here was sharper and brighter. There was something else too. A fantastic feeling that welled up inside me. I couldn't explain it so I stayed where I was and just enjoyed it. There was a building in the distance. It hugged the lower slopes of the mountain as if it was a part of the very landscape. A picture dropped into my head. I saw a wide, tree-lined street with houses on either side. The houses were unlike the tall, rectangular buildings I'd grown used to seeing on Earth. They were lower, with curvaceous designs that complemented the environment. Halfway along the road a house with a *limonge* tree growing in the front garden caught my eye. The tree's branches tapped gracefully against one window. In my vision I saw a girl, about twelve years old, with chestnut hair down to her waist, climb up the tree. As she disappeared into the upper branches the picture faded. Little Monkey! I bet she would make it to the top. A smile curved my lips until the ball dropped! I was that girl! I remembered that day as clearly as if it had been last week. I'd wanted to go swimming with my friends only Mariel had insisted I stayed home to meet her ancient aunt. I'd hung around until the aunt arrived. After the introductions, I'd asked if I could play in the garden. I'd hidden at the top of the tree until I was sure I'd been forgotten about. Then I'd run off to the lake to swim with my friends. There'd been hell to pay afterwards, but it had been worth it.

The feeling inside me intensified until suddenly I got what it was about. Happiness surged through me. I'd found my home.

Johnny lay a short distance away. His crumpled shape was an ugly blot on the immaculate landscape. In my mind I saw Carinna, the dark-haired, elfin-faced woman of my flashbacks. Her words rang out clearly in my ears.

'Never forget, our world is in your hands.'

Our world! Johnny wasn't welcome here. As I ran towards his prostrate body I stubbed my toe on his gun. I flinched, waiting for it to go off. Please don't let it blow me to pieces, especially not now! The gun spun harmlessly down the mountain, clattering loudly on the stones. Johnny opened his eyes.

'What happened? Where are we?' His bald head glistened with sweat.

I wasn't the only one bombing towards Johnny. The mountainside was alive with people, men and women. They poured out of the building, clapping their hands together as they ran. The sound, along with their pounding feet, made the hairs on my neck rise. A plethora of thoughts crashed into my mind.

No two people dressed alike in Pietra. We acted as a collective but were treated as individuals. We worked together for the greater good. Clapping warned of a danger.

Of course! Clapping was our way to warn of a danger. Now I knew why the applause at the music concert had freaked me out. Here, in Pietra, applause was given by standing in total silence.

It took a couple more seconds before I realised that Johnny was the cause of the clapping. Away to my left a man with a shock of red hair gunned towards me. He cupped his hands to his mouth and shouted, 'Amara!'

He sounded friendly, but there wasn't time to find out. It was my fault Johnny was here in Pietra. He was my responsibility. I dived and yanked him to his feet.

'Steady,' he moaned.

He was disorientated and unable to support himself. He slumped on me for support and I almost fell over.

My eyes scoured the mountainside for the *verbole*. There was nothing – except for a small fissure in the ground a couple of metres above us. It was little more than a large pothole. At first I dismissed it and continued to search for something more spectacular. But there was nothing else. Unconvinced, I dragged Johnny towards the fissure. I'd almost reached it before I felt something, a weak, magnetic force that radiated from the hole and drew me closer.

'*Halto!*'

It was extremely scary to see a bunch of people race towards you, especially when they were all clapping and yelling for you to stop. Red Head was in the lead and he waved at me.

'They're on your side!' I reminded myself. But Johnny was growing more alert. I had to get him back to Earth before he realised that we'd left his universe. We were a metre from the *verbole* when he suddenly dug his heels in the ground and refused to budge.

'Wait,' he shouted. 'What is that stuff?'

He dived to the ground and almost pulled me with him. 'Look, will you!' Johnny snatched up a handful of stones and stuffed them under my nose. 'Have you seen this?'

I recognised the stones immediately. The larger lumps,

veined with thick bands of gold, were white quartz. The smaller ones were solid gold pebbles. They covered the mountainside as thickly as moss grows on damp walls. Johnny was almost foaming at the mouth. 'You knew about this, didn't you? Greedy, when there's so much to go round.' He began to cram lumps of the quartz and gold pebbles into his pocket.

With a sense of shock, I realised that Nardo, Tor and Carinna hadn't exaggerated. Given the chance, the Johnnys of Earth would ruin Pietra. I had an alarming vision of how our planet might end up, if humans found out about it. They'd swarm here through the *verbole*, bringing machines to thump away at the landscape. They'd take our gold and leave the landscape barren and ugly.

'No!' I shouted. I flew at Johnny and beat him with my fists as I shoved him towards the wormhole.

'Get lost!' Johnny shoved me back. I fell and landed sprawled, face down on the ground. My hands stung and there was grit in my mouth. I spat it out and scrambled up again. My stomach was heavy with guilt. Johnny was the worst kind of a trespasser and I was to blame for his presence here. He'd never have found Pietra without me. I had to get him back to Earth, before he ruined everything.

Johnny darted around, muttering in delight, as he stuffed more rocks into his pockets. I grabbed at him.

He fought me savagely but I ducked away from the blows aimed at my head and shoulders. I jabbed my elbow in his stomach, kicking him hard in the back of his knees as he doubled up. He cursed me, using words that made me shudder in disgust. I had the advantage, though, and I used it to push him towards the *verbole*. We were half a metre away when the mountain seemed to unzip, exposing a cave. A small, roofless buggy hurtled from its depths. It was half the length of Dan's car and had wheels like enormous balls. The buggy rose up until it was a metre above the ground. It flew towards me. I charged at Johnny and rammed my shoulder into his side. He staggered forward and, lashing out with his hand, he whacked me on the head. I unsuccessfully shielded myself with my arms. Pain seared my skull, but I gritted my teeth and kneed him in the stomach. He yelped but continued to pick up rocks and stuff them in his already bulging pockets.

His greed made me sick. I grabbed his arm and dragged him the last few paces to the edge of the *verbole*. The magnetic force was much weaker than the one on Earth, but it was better than nothing. Johnny planted his feet in the ground and leaned back to resist it. I kept on shoving him until at last he lost his balance. He stepped forward, swearing violently as he wavered on the edge of the fissure. With one massive push I shoved him over.

The magnetic force sucked him in. The last thing I saw was Johnny's foot, spinning like water down a plughole. I laughed out loud with relief.

The flying buggy came closer. The blonde-haired boy, riding inside, didn't appear to be controlling it. He was using both of his hands to pull up the hood of a blue boiler suit. He shouted something and I wasn't sure if he was shouting at me, or the Guards. I didn't wait to find out. My immediate priority was to return to Earth and make sure Johnny stayed there. With a running jump, I launched myself into the *verbole*.

Blackness engulfed me. The lethal cold gnawed its way to the very core of my bones. I was shivering uncontrollably, so I went to wrap my arms round my body. But I couldn't move! To my horror I realised I was stuck in the position I'd assumed when I'd jumped into the *verbole*. Panic ballooned inside me. I concentrated on taking deep breaths, but I couldn't breathe either. I was stuck somewhere between life and death – not breathing but not suffocating. On and on I spun, with nothing around me but the impenetrable blackness.

It seemed ages before the air grew warmer. Flecks of light speckled the darkness. I began to fly upwards. Relief flooded through me; then suddenly I felt myself plummet. I hit the ground with a sickening crunch and rolled several metres before I stopped. My head was on fire; every bone in my body ached. I stared up. Dawn had arrived. The pale sky was streaked with pink. It was pretty but, after the splendour of the Pietran sky, the colours seemed washed out. I blinked a few times, but it didn't make any difference. This was as good as it got. I struggled to my feet and saw Johnny just a short distance away. His face was ashen and he lay in a pool of blood. I went over and examined him dispassionately. He was still breathing. He had a gash on his forehead. Luckily the amount of blood was disproportionate to the size of the wound.

Johnny's eyes flickered open. 'Help me up,' he groaned.

Hatred welled inside me. Why should I? He was nothing but a danger. My chest tightened as I struggled to work out what to do next. As a Pietran – a Watcher no less – it was my duty to protect our world. As a girl who'd lost her memory and lived on Earth as a human being, I strongly believed that memory reassembly was wrong. The seconds ticked by as I wrestled with my dilemma. It was the truth, cold and hard, that won out. Johnny knew too much. He had to be dealt with. I cringed as I slid the memory device out of my pocket. I really didn't want to do this. My hand was clammy and I couldn't get a proper grip on the applicator. With exaggerated care I passed the applicator to my left hand while I wiped my right on my jeans. My eyes swept over Johnny's torso in search of a patch of bare skin. Nardo had said it was best to use the neck. Johnny's neck was thick, squat and totally hairless. I held the memory device like a pen and, with trembling fingers, pressed it halfway between his ear and throat. I hated myself as I held it down.

'What's that?' Johnny's voice quivered with fear. His eyes rolled back in his head and then he passed out.

I almost fainted. Johnny's crumpled body seemed too still. Had I killed him? My breath came in ragged gasps as I bent to examine him.

TWENTY-TWO

To my relief Johnny was still breathing. I stuffed the memory device back in my pocket, sick with shame at what I'd done. There was a dull thud behind me. I spun round. Blue Suit had abandoned his flying buggy and followed me back through the wormhole.

'Amara, what happened? Are you okay?' He spoke in Pietran and his deep, lyrical voice stirred a memory.

'Yes, thanks. It's all under control.' I hoped he wouldn't notice how badly I was shaking.

'Who's he?' The Guard's eyes skimmed past Johnny.

More to the point, who are you? I knew his voice, but I just couldn't remember his name.

'Him, up there, who is he?' the Guard asked again.

I had a sudden sense of foreboding as I turned to look. I was still trying to place the Guard, but I wasn't prepared for the shock of seeing Dan. He stood a short distance away, beside an outcrop of rock. His face was tight and his feet rooted to the ground. He must have seen me administer the memory patch to Johnny. Worse still, it was clear that Dan thought that I'd killed him.

'I-it's not what you think,' I stuttered. I stepped

towards him.

Dan drew back, shielding himself behind the rocks.

'Dan, I can explain.'

I stepped closer, but he took off, sprinting up the mountain, his body taut with purpose.

'*Halto*!' Blue Suit went after him.

I came to my senses then and chased after them both. Blue Suit was fit and clearly used to the mountainous terrain. With every stride the gap between him and Dan closed. Rocks slithered under my feet. My heart pounded and I felt sick with fear. I had to stop Blue Suit from catching Dan.

'*Halto*!' I shouted in Pietran.

Blue Suit didn't falter. I sought for his name, convinced that I knew it, but the name stayed hidden in my black cavernous mind. Blue Suit caught Dan up and smoothly hooked an arm around his neck. Dan threw back his head and banged him in the face. Blood spurted from Blue Suit's nose; he punched Dan in the stomach. They wrestled together until they fell to the floor, where they continued to fight, grunting like trolls. I ran on, desperate to stop them, but my head was thumping and my legs felt weaker than clouds. Blue Suit reached into his pocket.

'No!' I screamed.

My legs wouldn't work. It felt like I was wading

through waist-high mud. It couldn't end like this. Dan was my friend. He didn't deserve to have his memories wiped. He was owed an explanation. Most of all I wanted say a proper goodbye. I wanted to tell him that I'd miss him and remember him always as my best friend here on Earth.

Blue Suit stood astride Dan, poised to administer a memory patch. Dan fought bravely back. Blue Suit was so much stronger, though. The muscles in his arm strained against his clothes as he brought the memory device down on Dan's neck.

'*Halto!*' I screamed. 'Don't hurt him!'

I reached Dan just as the device made contact with his skin. Dan feebly swatted it away. Blue Suit thrust again, but I was right behind him now. I snatched at his hood and yanked it back, exposing a mop of blonde hair and a long, muscular neck. I felt no regret as I slammed my memory device into his skin. Blue Suit twisted to face me and his blue eyes were numb with shock. A shard of ice pierced my heart. I couldn't breathe. Those eyes, those beautiful bright blue eyes… they belonged to the boy I'd kissed in my dream.

A whispered name floated like a feather inside my head. Faster than snowfall, the memories began to tumble into place. I reached inside my T-shirt and pulled out my amber necklace. The golden, spider's web chain glittered brightly. The amber stone flamed. The memories came faster. One was stronger than the rest, it replayed in my mind. It was my birthday. I was guest of honour at a special recital. We were in a building similar to the Margaret Becker, only it was bigger and much more beautiful. The concert stage overlooked a series of lakes, descending a hill in watery steps. A boy with blonde hair and sapphire blue eyes sat before a *grandatta pianato*. His face was full of passion as he played a love song that he'd composed especially for me. '*Amorra Mi*'. My song. He played the music through twice while I listened, along with a small group of family and close friends. As the final note died everyone stood in silent appreciation. My heart swelled with love and pride. The audience blurred as I stepped forward to hug the boy. He held me back as he reached into his jacket pocket and brought out a box. He opened it. An amber necklace sparkled up at me from its bed of dark velvet. The boy fastened the necklace around my neck and then pulled me into his arms.

'Something to remember me by,' he whispered. His lips brushed against my ear. 'In those long days when you are watching on Earth and I'm here guarding Pietra.' He drew me even closer and we kissed. It was just as it had been in my dream. As our lips moved together he murmured my name, over and over, 'Amara'.

The memory faded and suddenly it was his name that exploded from my lips in a scream.

'Marn!'

Marn's head lolled back. With his hand still clasped tightly around his memory device, he crumpled and fell on the ground. He lay there, comatose. I was paralysed with grief, but even then I couldn't help but compare him to Dan. The two boys were uncannily similar yet at the same time so very different. Marn was the sun and Dan the moon – and just like the sun and the moon, Marn would always shine more brightly.

An acid feeling burned in the bottom my stomach. It welled up and rose through my chest and into my throat. My nose tingled and I retched, over and over, until my stomach was empty and my muscles ached. Tears pooled in my eyes, and saliva ran from the side of my mouth. I groped in my pocket for a tissue and wiped away both the spit and the sweat on my face. I felt drained. There was a foul taste in my mouth and my head ached.

'I'm sorry,' I whispered. I stroked Marn's suntanned face. '*Amorra mi*, I'm so sorry.'

Fear paralysed my brain. All I could think about was Marn waking and not being able to remember me. Was there a greater irony than for my *amoretta* to lose his memories, just as I was regaining mine?

A hand on my shoulder made me gasp. 'Dan!' I wheeled round to face him.

'Have you killed him too?' Dan's eyes were glazed like a sleepwalker.

'No! I haven't killed anyone.' How could he think that of me? But with Marn sprawled on the ground, lying so still that it was impossible to tell if he was breathing, maybe it wasn't so difficult.

My heart hammered against my chest. What if more Pietrans came through the *verbole*? How long before the Earth-side Guards discovered us? 'You have to get out of here.'

'I'm not going anywhere until you tell me what's going on. No secrets, you promised. Remember?'

'No secrets, I promise. Only I can't tell you anything here. It's too dangerous. You have to go before they find you.'

'I'm staying put. Whoever they are, I won't let them harm you.'

'I'm not the one in danger. You are. It's complicated. I'll explain everything later, but right now you have to trust me and go. *Please.*'

Dan reached out and took both my hands in his. 'No! Whatever this is, we're in it together.'

We weren't though, not any more. 'Please, Dan, just go. You're lucky they haven't caught you already. The Guards are professionals.'

A ghost of a smile lit Dan's face. 'I know there are Guards.'

My eyes raked the mountainside. It was only a matter of time before someone discovered us here. Then everything would be over. What chance did I stand against Tor and his men? There was only one way left to save Dan.

'Go,' I said harshly. 'Or you're next.' I waved the memory device at him. 'You'd kill me too?' Dan was almost too stunned to speak.

I went to correct him then stopped. Let him think what he liked, if it got rid of him.

Dan eyes pleaded with mine. I held his gaze without flinching, even though it tore me apart.

'You'd really kill me?' A muscle twitched in his jaw. 'I trusted you, Amber.' Abruptly he turned and walked away.

I wanted to call out and tell him to be careful, that the danger wasn't over and he should stay hidden as he made his way back to town. I didn't dare, though. I couldn't let him know that I cared about his safety, or he'd guess my bluff. I watched him jog away until finally he disappeared into the trees. By then I couldn't stand up any longer.

Shooting pains needled my skull. I felt sick with giddiness. I needed to lie down. I lowered myself to the ground and cradled my head on my arms. It was very uncomfortable, but it helped stem the nausea.

I must have blacked out. The next thing I remember, someone was gently shaking me awake. At first my eyes wouldn't focus. My senses told me I wasn't in my Waterside room, but I couldn't work out where I was.

'Amara, are you okay?' Nardo's voice brought everything rushing back. Misery punched my stomach. I'd messed up. Marn, my *amoretta*, was lying unconscious, possibly with a damaged memory. Dan, my best friend here on Earth, hated me. It couldn't get any worse.

Nardo pushed a strand of hair from my face. I grabbed his hand and weakly gripped his fingers.

'Can you sit up?' Tor leaned over me.

I bit the inside of my cheek to stop myself from groaning out loud as he and Nardo helped me into a sitting position. They removed their fleeces and used them as padding as they propped me against a boulder.

'What happened? How did Marn get here?'

Guilt almost suffocated me. 'Johnny,' I whispered. 'He came after me. There was a struggle. We fell through the *verbole*.'

'What?' Both Tor and Nardo were aghast. 'You went

through the *verbole* without wearing a travel suit?'

'And Johnny, but I brought him straight back and gave him a memory patch. He's over there, comatose.'

'By the love of Pietra! What were you thinking?' Tor's eyes blazed with fury. 'Two journeys in the *verbole*, back to back without the mandatory time lag and without wearing a protective suit – the effects of magnetic energy could have killed you!'

So that's why I felt like I'd been dancing with death. Nardo had mentioned travel suits, not that it would have made any difference at the time. 'We fell,' I protested. 'Johnny held a gun to me.'

Nardo gripped my arm. 'Are you wounded?'

I shook my head and immediately wished I hadn't. My brain must have slipped anchor from the way it was crashing against my skull. 'The gun, it's still in Pietra.'

'The Pietran side Guards will find it. They'll dispose of it safely. Why's Marn here? What happened to him?'

I looked at Marn, who lay a short distance from me, and then at Johnny, sprawled on his back like a dead rat. Guilt twisted my tongue. I had to fight it to avoid blurting out the truth. 'I didn't know that Marn had followed us back to Earth. I was putting a memory patch on Johnny when he arrived. Johnny was struggling and Marn got in the way just as I applied the patch. At first I thought he was fine. He ran off shouting. I dealt with Johnny and when I'd finished…' The words stuck in my throat. 'Marn, he wasn't good. He sort of fell down.'

'That's bad.'

A sob rose in my throat. 'You said it was harmless! I remember Marn. He's my *amoretta*. What if I've destroyed all his memories?'

'You won't have.' Nardo hugged me. 'Memory patches are harmless. They wipe the memory of anything unusual. So you and Johnny arriving in Pietra would be unusual, as would you administering Marn with a memory patch. When Marn wakes he won't have a clue where he is or how he got here. It's fantastic that you remember him.' Nardo's face shone with happiness.

Pain was splitting my head in two. I massaged my forehead. 'What if it doesn't work properly? You said there'd been accidents.'

'On people,' said Nardo. 'Their brains are different from ours.'

Tor's face was saying something different. 'In the early stages, when the memory drug was being developed, we tested it on Pietrans and there were a few accidents,' he said, carefully. 'But these test cases were Pietrans who refused to conform to our way of life. You could say the accidents occurred because their brains weren't operating on the same wavelength as a normal Pietran. In every society there are rogues. Marn's a fine upstanding citizen. It's highly unlikely that he'll suffer any adverse effects from the memory drug.'

'But it's not impossible?'

'Nothing's impossible,' said Tor heavily.

Bile rose in my mouth. It burned my throat as I swallowed it down. What if I had damaged Marn's memories? I would never forgive myself.

TWENTY-THREE

Tor sent me back to the *portacasa* with Nardo. I protested like mad. I wanted to stay with Marn, but apparently you didn't argue with a superior.

'I'll overlook your insubordination this time. You've taken two trips in the *verbole*, without the appropriate protective clothing, so it's natural that you are not yourself.' Tor's reprimand was spoken gently. 'Go and rest. You need to be in top condition to enable us to execute your exit from Earth without arousing suspicion. If the plan goes wrong, then we'll be looking at mass memory reassembly.'

Nardo put his arm around me as he led me away. 'Don't worry about Marn. He'll wake up with a sore head and he'll probably feel confused. When he finds out what happened he's bound to laugh it off. You know he will.'

I knew Marn had a great sense of humour, but what if the memory drug went wrong on him? What if... I was obsessing and it wasn't helpful. To change the subject I asked, 'What's going to happen to Johnny now?'

'The Guards will transport him back to town and leave him near Robert. When both men wake, and see all the empty bottles that we've planted around them, they'll naturally assume that they've been sleeping off a bad hangover.'

I'd taken a few reluctant steps towards the *portacasa* when I remembered something. 'Wait! Johnny's pockets are full of quartz and gold pebbles that he took when we were in Pietra.'

'*Shizatt!*' Nardo swore. 'Can you stand on your own for a minute?'

I nodded. I was feeling much better and didn't need his help any more, but it was nice to have his arm round me. My memories of Nardo were still a blank. I liked him, though, and I was beginning to feel a connection between us. Nardo ran back to Tor and together they emptied Johnny's pockets. Afterwards Nardo conducted a mental search of Johnny, using his telekinetic skills. As I watched Johnny's clothes ripple from Nardo's mind touch I felt strangely reassured. Nardo would leave no stone unturned – literally! Imagine if a pebble or piece of quartz had been left behind in Johnny's pocket. Its presence would seriously jeopardise the safety of our world. Tor counted the rocks and golden pebbles they'd extracted from Johnny and when Nardo got back to the *portacasa* he counted them again, to make sure that he hadn't lost any en route. Then he locked them away in a safe that was concealed in the kitchen floor.

Nardo made breakfast. I sat and played with mine, a white Earth cube that had melted into something resembling yoghurt and fruit. A short while later Tor joined us. He refused food but accepted a mug of hot water with a slice of *limonge*. He cradled the mug in his hands as he debriefed me. He made me recount everything that had happened out on the mountain, in such minuscule detail, that I had to think very hard about what I said. Eventually, Tor seemed satisfied, but he still proceeded to give me another lecture on the importance of the Confidentiality Decree. I felt as if he didn't quite trust me. Or maybe I was suffering from a guilty conscience.

Immediately after my debriefing, Tor and Nardo started an intense discussion on the state of the security around the Earth-side *verbole*.

'We need more Guards and they need to be stationed much closer to the *verbole*,' said Tor.

'What about the mandatory distance?' Nardo argued. 'If we allow the Guards to work any closer to the *verbole*, they'll be exposed to too much radiation. They won't be able to do their jobs properly if they get sick. '

'They can work closer if we make the shifts shorter,' Tor argued.

I rested my elbows on the table, with my hands

supporting my chin, and let the argument float over my head. The day I'd woken up in hospital with no memory would stay with me for the rest of my life. It had seemed like the most terrifying thing that had ever happened to me. At the time I thought that life couldn't have got any worse. Only now it had. I hated the thought of Marn lying unconscious on the mountainside, especially when it was my fault. Marn needed me by his side, a familiar face when he woke. There hadn't been enough spare guards to carry him back to the *portacasa* straight away, but Tor had promised me that in the meantime he'd check on him frequently. I was terrified that Marn would wake when he was alone. Please let him remember who he was. Marn and I were good together. The best! I refused to contemplate a future without him.

Then there was Dan. No wonder I'd been attracted to him. In many ways he was so like Marn. Dan had risked his life for me, and I'd always be grateful for that, but what of our friendship? Did it have a future? I didn't know. One thing I was certain about, though. Dan thought I was a killer and his misconception could jeopardise everything.

I had a duty to come clean and confess my sins to Tor. He could easily contain the situation, by performing a memory reassembly on Dan and everyone he'd shared my secrets with.

No! How could I even think that! I slammed my treacherous thoughts away, shut them in a box and stood on the lid. Dan, his family and all my friends at Waterside deserved better treatment from me. My time on Earth, living as a human, had taught me things that Pietrans didn't understand. You couldn't paint every person with the same brush. Individuals, governments even, were greedy. They started wars and caused pollution. But there was a greater number of humans who were kind and compassionate. I was convinced that if we, the Pietrans, shared our technological advances and knowledge with humans, there could be a better future for Earth. It didn't have to be the one of self-destruction that Nardo had prophesised. There was a brighter future that humans would sign up to, if they were properly educated to the benefits.

I was suddenly even keener to return to my home planet. From my experiences so far, I reasoned, that once I was there, my memories would flood back. Then I would ask the *medicio* to pronounce me fit to return to Earth. My work here wasn't done. I'd lived as a human. That made me unique. I had a more intimate knowledge of human behaviour than anyone else on my planet. Somehow, I had to make Pietrans see that humans were intrinsically good, that we had a duty to show them how to conserve their world. What they did with that knowledge was their prerogative. But at least we would have tried to help, rather than stand back and let the Earth be destroyed.

'How about it, Amara?' Tor's voice broke into my thoughts. 'You've been through so much. I'd feel much happier if you rested a while. Stay here for another night, before you return to Waterside. It would give Nardo some extra time to refresh your training.'

Tor wanted me to stay for another night? It was a tempting idea. I'd be around when Marn woke. It might make a difference to how his memory coped with the after-effects of the drug, if I was here in person. I was about to agree to his suggestion when I remembered Dan. I needed to see him quickly. I had to tell him what had happened out there on the mountain, before he told people what he thought he'd seen. The safety of Pietra was in my hands. No exaggeration. My head and my heart wanted two very different things. I wrestled with my decision, but I was a Watcher. My head won out.

'I have to go back now. Mia and Jeff are expecting me. There'll be too many awkward questions if I stay away any longer.'

Tor studied me for a moment, his face unreadable, then he nodded, 'Yes, you're right. It's best that we get this over and done with quickly. You shouldn't be here.

You need to be back in Pietra, where we can get you to a *medicio*, one who specialises in the brain.' He stopped abruptly and a muscle twitched in his jaw.

I knew he was thinking of Nell. I changed the subject by asking him a question. 'What happened to Holly?'

'She's been dealt with. She won't cause you any more problems.'

Poor Holly! Even though she was such a cow I couldn't help feeling a little bit sorry for her. Like Nell and me, she was a victim too: wrong place, wrong time.

Tor raised a smile then he patted my arm. 'Keep it up, Amara. You're doing a great job.'

I wondered if he'd still be smiling if he knew the truth.

A short while later Nardo accompanied me back to Balochry so I could catch the train to Edinburgh. He insisted on talking me all the way to the train station. 'Look after yourself,' he said breathlessly, as we parted. He sounded as if he was scared to let me go.

'I will.'

'I'll come for you as soon as we can. The paperwork's almost ready. I'm in the middle of making a credit card, to hire a car. Then it will just be a case of contacting your social worker. It shouldn't take more than twenty-four hours.'

Nardo's concern made me smile. I'd lived incognito

at Waterside for weeks. I had only one day left there. It would have been fun, if Marn hadn't been comatose, and Dan didn't hate me.

Just before I'd left the *portacasa* the Guards had changed shifts. For a short while there'd been enough of them to move Marn off the mountainside and into a bed. Tor let me see him for five Earth minutes. He'd looked so peaceful as he lay sleeping on a bunk bed. I'd longed to run my fingers through his rumpled blonde hair, to kiss his eyelids and the long dark lashes brushing his cheeks. It was awkward with Tor there, watching. I stroked Marn's cheek and whispered softly in his ear, '*Etta tu amorra. Recordia mia.*' I love you. Remember me.

'It's not a problem,' I reassured Nardo, now. 'I lived at Waterside for weeks without knowing who I was. This will be easy.'

'I'm so proud of you.' Nardo squeezed my arm and again I was racked with guilt.

The train was packed. I found myself squeezed on a seat next to a bearded man who was dressed for hiking. He held a dirty rucksack on his lap. He wanted to talk and, pulling a map from the bag, proudly informed me that he'd been climbing in the mountains for weeks. He showed me the route he'd taken. I nodded and tried not to breathe too deeply. He smelled like he hadn't taken a bath for weeks either. I spent most of the journey hoping that he'd get off the train, or stop talking and let me think. It was just my luck that he was going all the way to Edinburgh. In the end, though, he turned out to be a good thing. Edinburgh station was huge and daunting. I didn't have a clue where to go to catch the bus. He gave me directions to the bus station. In no time at all, I'd navigated my way through the hoards of travellers and joined a queue for the Kirkgreen bus.

I was more nervous than a Watcher should ever admit to. For something to do I pulled my mobile out of my pocket and checked to see if I had any messages. Unsurprisingly there were none. I fiddled with the keypad while I wondered whether to send Dan a text and tell him that I was on my way back. It probably wasn't a great idea, so I settled for texting Lucy instead. In the quarter of an hour wait for the bus I texted Lucy three more times. She didn't reply. I checked my phone every few minutes but the screen remained a big, fat blank. It didn't improve my nerves or help my churning stomach. Why hadn't Lucy texted me back? Was she ignoring me? Had Dan told her that I'd tried to kill him? When I returned to Waterside I could be walking into a trap. The police, or army even, might be there, waiting to arrest me. I bet they'd have guns. I was an alien, after all.

It was a relief when the bus arrived. I waited for a group of passengers to disembark before I shuffled on board. The seats were dirty and worn and the bus smelled worse than an old shed. A memory of a shiny pod, that hovered half a metre above the ground, with comfortable chairs and an invisible force field that acted like seat belts in a car, flashed through my mind. The buses in Pietra seemingly were much more sophisticated than this one. The journey took thirty-five minutes. It was late afternoon when the bus trundled into Kirkgreen. There was still no word from Lucy and nothing from Nardo either. I'd secretly hoped that he might text me with an update on Marn. The knot of fear in my stomach pulled tighter as I stepped off the bus and watched it pull away. A new, unwelcome scenario, to explain Lucy's silence, popped into my head. What if Dan hadn't returned to Waterside and was lying unconscious somewhere, a victim of memory reassembly? My breath stuck in my throat. Worse still, what if Tor had somehow learned that I hadn't been truthful with him? What if he'd beaten me back and *dealt* with all of my friends?

My fingers were trembling as I punched out Lucy's number. Her mobile rang for ages then, with a click, it switched to voicemail. A mechanical voice invited me to leave a message so that Lucy could call me back.

There didn't seem much point. I disconnected the call and went into the newsagent to ask for the number of the local taxi firm.

A shop assistant directed me back outside to look in the window for something she called 'the wee ads'. I bought a bottle of mineral water and a sandwich first. I opted for the cheese salad even though, having been exposed to meat, I'd have preferred the chicken. I wasn't hungry. I was anxious and thoroughly bored of hanging around, but eating a sandwich was better than doing nothing in the long wait for the taxi to arrive. Thankfully, the taxi driver was the silent type. I stared out of the window and a short while later I saw the wooden sign for the Waterside School of Music.

'That's it!' My heart raced and my hands felt clammy.

The taxi driver turned off the road and the car bounced along the potholed drive. The afternoon sun streamed in through the open windows. With it came a fresh woodland scent that reminded me of Marn. The road curved, the trees thinned and there was Loch Calness. Sailing boats swooped across the water, their sails billowing like enormous wings. My heart dipped and a warm feeling stole through me. I loved it here. For one brief moment I was filled with a deep contentment.

TWENTY-FOUR

The taxi pulled up in the car park. I was busy taking money from my purse and it wasn't until I handed the driver a ten-pound note that I saw the police car parked in the corner. My heart smacked against my ribs. Dan had betrayed me. Unaware of my terror, the driver rummaged in a small leather bag for change. I waved it away, 'Keep it,' I said. 'Thanks for the ride.'

'You're welcome, lass.'

I felt totally exposed as I climbed out of the car and walked swiftly across the car park. The taxi disappeared down the drive and I pressed myself up against the trunk of a tall pine. Carinna's voice sounded in my head, low and calm.

First rule, assess.

The police car was parked close to Melody House so I thought that's where its occupants had gone. Mia and Jeff had an office, with French windows that opened on to a kind of porch along one side of the house. The office was where they conducted most of their business. I checked that there was no one watching before I ran from the tree to the garage where I pressed myself up against the wall.

From here, I had a clear view into the office. The French windows were open and I could hear the low rumble of voices. It was impossible to make out words, but I was reassured by the calm, rhythmic cadence. There was no panic yet. I crept closer and concealed myself behind a sprawling bush with waxy, dark green leaves. Mia and Jeff were seated with their backs to the door. Two police officers, a woman and a man, faced them. There was a third person in the room. I was unable to identify who it was, so I shifted my weight and leaned forward for a better view. A hand clamped over my mouth. A muscular arm snaked around my waist and pulled me backwards. I lost my balance and fell against a man's solid chest. He dragged me away. My neck snapped back and a strand of my hair got trapped under his arm and pinched my scalp. My attacker dragged me deeper into the bush. My heart raced, but my mind stayed sharp and focused. One of Carinna's lessons in self-defence came back to me.

When being strangled, your natural instinct is to pull away. DON'T! Lean into your attacker and bring your heel down hard on the top of his foot. At the same time bend forward and shove him off with your buttocks.

As I leaned back into my assailant's arms he went rigid then he shoved me away, as if he couldn't bear to be that close to me. I bit his hand and he swore softly. I bit him again and this time he pressed the heel of his palm hard against my lips so I bit myself instead. Twigs snapped and crackled under my feet. I cast around for one with some substance. A large one, with the kink in the middle, was perfect. I fixed it with my mind.

Up.

With jerky movements, that matched my breathing, the stick rose from the ground. I made it go higher. When it disappeared behind my attacker's back I held a picture of it in my mind. I twisted my head and a short while later saw the stick rise above his shoulders. I couldn't hold the position and had to use a little guesswork when I swung it down on his head. My guess was good. The blow sent him reeling. He pitched forward and smashed his chin on the top of my head. We fell together and the breath rushed out of me as we landed. He was on top and his muscular body forced me into the gritty ground.

'Get off.' The words hissed through my clenched teeth.

'Stop struggling then!' He flipped me onto my back and pinned my arms to my side as he glared down at me.

'Dan!' So who was the other person in the office with his parents and the police?

'What are you dong here?' he demanded. His eyes were colder than a glacier.

'You reported me.' I couldn't help the note of

disappointment that coloured my voice. On the ride back from Balochry I'd nursed a tiny flame of hope that Dan would come to his senses and realise that I could never kill anyone. With that flame now extinguished I felt hollow inside. I was too late. Dan had spilled my secrets. I'd have to confess my sins to Tor, who'd undoubtedly arrange for a mass memory wipe. So many innocent people!

And what if my other nightmare came to fruition? Marn. Would there be anything left to live for, if his memory was wiped clean?

'I'm sorry.' The words did nothing to convey how deeply I meant them.

'You're sorry?' Dan was incredulous.

'I didn't kill anyone. You shouldn't have reported me. I tried to warn you, but it's too late now. Locking me up won't solve anything. Nardo will be here soon. When he finds out what's happened, that you've told people about me, he'll call for a mass memory wipe. It doesn't hurt, although you'll probably feel groggy for a while afterwards. It's harmless...' I stopped.

'Amber, you're not making sense! Who's going to lock you up?'

'The police are. You called for the police.'

'No, I didn't. The police are here to see Lucy. Someone tried to mug her in Kirkgreen.'

'Really?' The relief made me dizzy. Almost as an afterthought I added, 'Poor Lucy. Was she hurt?'

'She's fine. They didn't get her bag, but Mum reported the incident anyway to help prevent another attack.'

'So why did you jump on me?'

'Why do you think? After what happened earlier, I then find you creeping round the side of our house. It's hardly the actions of a normal, law-abiding person.'

'It's not what you think. Look, can we go somewhere more private? How about we walk down by the loch?'

'You want me to walk by the loch with you, on my own?' A hard edge crept back into Dan's voice. 'Yeah, right! If you don't mind I'd rather stay here where it's more public.'

'Johnny and Marn, they're not dead.' I spoke quickly with my eyes fixed on Dan's to show that I had nothing to hide. 'I gave them a drug to make them forget certain things they'd seen. Like the way I can move things with my mind. The drug's harmless, well normally,' I added as I remembered the promise I'd made to tell Dan the truth. 'I drugged Johnny and Marn to stop them from telling the Guards about you.'

Dan stared at me blankly.

'Look, it's complicated and highly secret. Please Dan, I need to be sure that we won't be overheard. You can tell Mia that you're going for a walk with me if you don't trust me, but if I wanted to kill you, don't you think I'd have done it this morning? No one would have found your body in the mountains,' I said wearily.

Dan studied me for a moment then his lips twitched. 'All right,' he said grudgingly. He helped me up and waited while I brushed the dirt from my clothes and picked the twigs from my hair. We walked in silence, our feet crunching softly on old leaves, as we made our way around the back of the garden to the loch. As we came out into the open my breath caught in my throat. It wasn't Pietra but it was still beautiful here. The sun, in a cerulean sky, rippled the water and made it sparkle. I stood for a moment to absorb the view. Dan walked quickly on, without checking to see if I could keep up, as he led the way to a secluded spot at the far end of the loch. There, he leaned against the trunk of a tree, with roots that paddled in the silver blue water like gnarled toes.

My heart hammered so fast that I could hardly breathe. 'The thing is,' I said in a rush. 'I'm not from this world. I'm an alien, a kind of anthropologist from the planet Pietra. We call ourselves Watchers. We've been coming here for years to study you.'

'What?' Dan was taken aback and he sounded annoyed. 'I guessed that you were from another world but I thought it was your first visit here. If you've been here before then why haven't your people made contact with us? Don't you think it would have been nice to introduce yourselves? We might want to study you too.'

'It's not that simple.' It was hard to explain when I wasn't totally convinced of the philosophy myself. 'You saw Johnny and Robert's reaction to me. We don't want to start a war. Your world is divided into countries, right?' Nardo had taught me some facts about Earth when he'd refreshed my training. 'You spy on other countries, to help keep the peace?'

Dan picked at a flaky piece of bark. 'Well, yes, I suppose we do.'

'Then it's the same for us. Pietra is one place. It's not divided up into individual countries. We've known for ages that we're linked to Earth by wormholes, so to ensure there's peace between our worlds we spy on you.' I omitted to tell him how we'd used that knowledge to advance our own standard of living. It wasn't something I was proud of.

'Back there, in the mountains, I never meant to harm you. I was trying to make you leave. Pietran law dictates that no Earth person must know about us. If we'd been caught together they'd have forced a memory drug on you, to make you forget me. You've been a good friend,

Dan. The best! You deserve more than that.'

Dan chiselled away at the tree trunk until he levered up a large splinter of wood. 'I've *been* a good friend, meaning that you're not staying?'

'I was supposed to be here for nine months, but because of the accident and losing my memory, I'm being sent home. Nardo, he's my brother, will be here to collect me soon.' My voice sounded like dry leaves rustling in the breeze. 'There's something else. I've got an *amoretta*, a boyfriend, called Marn. I remember him now.'

I stood very still and watched Dan as he lined the splinter up with the tip of his finger. Then he flicked it into the loch. He met my gaze evenly. 'Marn, he was the one in the blue boiler suit? He was also the one who tried to give me the memory drug.'

I nodded.

'Only you drugged him first?'

I hesitated. Should I tell Dan the truth? That I hadn't remembered Marn until *after* I'd drugged him. I'd promised to be totally honest with him, but on this occasion did it really matter? I'd already broken so many rules of the Confidentiality Decree to protect Dan. There didn't seem much point in having a '*but what would you have done if you had recognised Marn?*' discussion.

Dan smiled suddenly then pushed himself off the tree

trunk. He stepped closer and to my great surprise he put his arms round me. He dropped his face down to mine until his lips were so close that I could almost taste them.

'So this is goodbye?' he whispered.

'Yes.'

Dan dipped his head and his lips met mine. He kissed me quickly, the kiss of a close friend. I closed my eyes and kissed him lightly back. A warm glow spread through me as I stepped away.

'When we were in Balochry, outside the café, I was about to ask you out, but now I'm glad I didn't.' Dan sounded wistful.

'No?' I said, bristling. 'Why? Was my kissing that bad?'

'No.' Dan shook his head sadly. 'It was after you pushed me away that I realised how unfair I'd been. It wasn't right to ask you to be my girlfriend in the moments before you were about to find out who you were. I think I've always known that you'd have a boyfriend. You're special, Amber. Anyone can see that. And now there's another reason. On the drive home from Balochry, I reached an important decision.' He took a deep breath and said slowly, as if it was something he wanted to try out for size, 'I'm going away.'

'You are?'

'Yes. I'm applying to Plymouth University, for a place

on the Architecture course. I'm going to apply for a deferred place so that I can take a gap year first, to travel.'

'What about your mum and dad? What about all this?' I waved my hand at the loch.

'It's like I said before, Mum and Dad will be disappointed, but they'll get over it. They'd be far more disappointed if I didn't follow my heart. They'd never force me to stay here and run this place if they knew that I wanted to do something different. I should have been more honest with them when I finally realised this wasn't what I wanted.'

'Oh, Dan! Good luck with it. You'll love travelling.' I was glad he was moving on too. It made me feel less guilty. 'I'll never forget you...' I stopped talking because my voice had started to squeak.

'I'll remember you too. Whereever I am, whenever the stars are shining, I'll look up and I'll know that you're out there somewhere.'

Suddenly my eyes were swimming in hot tears. I blinked them back and reached for Dan's hand. I held it tightly. If things had been different... but I had Marn and he was my true soulmate. My guilt was so much lighter for knowing that Dan was about to embark on his own adventure.

I spent a bittersweet evening with my friends. We

played volleyball down by the lake. Holly was there too. She wasn't exactly nice to me, but she didn't make any of her usual bitchy remarks either. I was sad to be leaving. I decided that I hated goodbyes, and hanging around made it much worse. Mostly though, I wanted to get back to Marn. He had to remember me. What would I do if he didn't?

Nardo came for me early the following morning. He arrived at the same time as Nicky. My social worker had wanted to see me, not just to sort out the legalities involved before she handed me over to my brother, but also to say a proper goodbye. I felt like a traitor as I hugged Mia, Jeff, Lucy, Josh, Amy and Ellie, George and, lastly, Dan goodbye and promised to keep in touch, when I knew that I couldn't. Nardo seemed surprised by the warmth of everyone's farewell wishes. It was the first thing he mentioned when we were finally in the hire car and bouncing away down the drive.

'You've made a big impression in the few weeks that you've been here. They all seemed genuinely sad to see you go.'

I sat back, slipped off my trainers and propped my feet up on the dashboard.

'Not all humans are bad. Living as a human has taught me far more about them than I could ever learn through watching them from a distance. I've had a unique experience.'

'Well, I'm sure the *Polittica* will be very interested to hear all about it,' said Nardo, as he slowed for the end of the drive.

I smiled to myself as he pulled out onto the main road. I was sure that the *Polittica* would be interested in my findings. But I was going to have my work cut out to convince them to let me action the plans I had for my subsequent visits to Earth.

'How's Marn? Has he forgiven me?' My casual tone belied the pounding of my heart.

'He's fine,' said Nardo. 'He'll be gone by the time we get back.'

'Gone?'

'Back to Pietra.' Nardo glanced at me. 'What? Surely you didn't expect him to stay for a chat? This is a job, Amara, not a holiday.'

'I know, it's just... So he was fine, then. No side effects?'

'Apart from a colossal headache, he was the same old Marn,' said Nardo. 'He was very shocked and upset to learn about you and Nell.'

Relief bubbled like spring water in my veins. My fears were unfounded. Marn was fine and he remembered me.

I was so desperate to see him again I could hardly sit still. I reached for my amber necklace and held the stone all the way back to Balochry.

Several hours later, I stood about a metre from the *verbole*. I was dressed in a bright orange travel suit and its oversized hood completely covered my head. It was light and comfortable and, amazingly, the silky material negated the effects of the radiation. The last time I'd come here I'd felt dizzy and sick and unable to think clearly. Now my mind was racing through all the instructions Nardo had given me about my imminent journey. I glanced across at Tor, dressed in a similar suit in a deep shade of red. He was going back to Pietra because of Nell. He needed time to come to terms with his terrible loss.

He smiled back at me. 'Ready?'

I looked up at the mountains. They soared above me, their peaked heads nudging the rose-washed evening sky. It was beautiful here, so totally unspoilt. It was hard to believe that one day, if left to humans, Earth was headed for destruction. There had to be something my planet could do to help. I didn't doubt that it would be a challenge. You couldn't force a lifestyle change on people against their will. But with education and a willingness to share another's perspective the challenge wasn't insurmountable. And I wasn't just talking about humans.

Pietrans had a lot to learn too. I couldn't wait to go home, but I knew I would definitely come back. I'd broken the rules and made friends here. Friends who'd helped me unconditionally and without any sort of judgement. I owed them.

I took a last, long look around and committed the scene to memory. I'd been working hard to build a new set of memories ever since the accident. 'I'm ready.'

Tor and I stepped up to the edge of the *verbole* together.

'On the count of three,' he said. '*Una*, *dua*, *tiree*.'

As one we jumped into the void. It was blacker than I'd remembered, but I was snug in my suit and couldn't feel the bone-gnawing cold, or crushing force that had beaten the life out of me the last time I'd travelled this way. It seemed like hardly any time had passed before I saw ribbons of light flickering towards me. I was catapulted towards a sparkling blue sky. My suit inflated. It filled with a cushioning layer of air that allowed me to float to the ground. I landed neatly, both feet together, a short way from the *verbole*. Out of the corner of my eye I saw Tor land a few paces to my left. He raised a hand to me and I raised mine back. I pushed back my hood and drank in the raw, unspoilt beauty of the Pietran mountains.

'Amara.'

In the distance I saw a boy standing in front of a building

that almost grew out of the mountainside. His blonde hair shone like a halo in the bright sun. He shouted my name again.

'Marn!' My voice echoed around the mountains.

I ran towards him. Marn laughed as he caught me. He lifted me up and swung me round. My hair spun out behind and bound us together in a silky chestnut rope.

'You're back.' He held my face in his hands and kissed me hard on the lips.

A fiery heat pulsed through every part of me. As I looked up into Marn's bright blue eyes, I thought I might burst with love. '*Etta tu amorra*,' I whispered.

I pulled him closer as we kissed again, a slow kiss that left me shaking with desire. Marn and I were together. I'd come home.

Acknowledgements

I used to think that writing a book was the result of one person's work, but nothing is further from the truth. There's practically a village full of people working behind the scene, to bring a writer's work to the bookshelf.

So many people have been involved in breathing life into Amber. My heartfelt thanks must go firstly to the wonderful team at Curious Fox, especially Catherine Clarke, Laura Knowles and my brilliant editor, Vaarunika Dharmapala. Thanks Vaarunika, for gently pushing me that extra mile and then making me go one further.

Thanks also to my agent Pat White and to Claire Wilson. I hope you know how much I value you both.

To my friends, who forgive me when I don't return their calls. I'm sorry for all the times I've let you down because I've been too immersed in Amber to spend time with you in the real world.

Antonia MacPhee, Lee Weatherly and Linda Chapman, my first readers. Love and thanks for giving me such honest, wise and helpful feedback. Thanks also to Lee, Linda and Val Wilding for regular emails and coffee dates. You make me laugh and stop me from hurling my computer out of the window on the bad days.

Love and thanks also to Will MacPhee for fantastic 24/7 techie support, and for fixing my PC after its spectacular demise when I was writing *Amber*; Tim MacPhee for regular dog walking; and to Mum, Dad and Sarah, for being there.

And lastly to Alistair, who married me for my postcards and ended up with a library, LYB.

About the author

Julie Sykes has always made things up, but it was a holiday in Jersey that inspired her to write down her stories. She is now the author of many books, including the best-selling Silver Dolphins series. *Amber* is her first book for older readers.

Julie once lived on a fish farm, sharing her home with 300,000 rainbow trout. She now lives in the south of England with her family, their pet wolf and a few goldfish.

You can find out more about Julie at
www.juliesykes.co.uk

For more exciting books from
brilliant authors, follow the fox!
www.curious-fox.com